PRAISE FOR
ELIZABETH QUINN'S
MURDER MOST GRIZZLY

"Exceptional. . . . Absorbing. . . . Quinn makes excellent use of the arctic landscape. With its wild beauty and natural dangers, isolation and cultural diversity, and ecological issues and animal lore, it is proving to be a dramatic setting for crime fiction."

—Gail Pool, *Wilson Public Library*

"*Murder Most Grizzly* offers some timely information and insights on the Alaskan ecology and introduces [Dr. Lauren Maxwell], a likable and competent new female sleuth, who's as passionate about the environment as about getting her man."

—*The Purloined Letter*

"Most readers will . . . get a great deal of enjoyment out of *Murder Most Grizzly.*"

—Kathi Maio, *New York Newsday*

"[An] intriguing and unusual murder mystery. . . . Lauren Maxwell is an intelligent and feisty female protagonist. . . . There's plenty of suspense, sharp dialogue and more than enough 'grizzly' facts as Lauren . . . learns just how puny a defense a .45-caliber Colt is against an angry *Ursa arctos horribilis.*"

—Jane Missett, *Blade-Citizen Preview* (Oceanside, CA)

AVAILABLE FROM POCKET BOOKS

Also by Elizabeth Quinn

Any Day Now
Blood Feud
Murder Most Grizzly
A Wolf in Death's Clothing

Published by POCKET BOOKS

A LAUREN MAXWELL MYSTERY

A WOLF IN DEATH'S CLOTHING

ELIZABETH QUINN

POCKET BOOKS

New York   London   Toronto   Sydney   Tokyo   Singapore

This book is a work of fiction. Names, characters, places and incidents are products of the author's imagination or are used fictitiously. Any resemblance to actual events or locales or persons, living or dead, is entirely coincidental.

An *Original* Publication of POCKET BOOKS

POCKET BOOKS, a division of Simon & Schuster Inc.
1230 Avenue of the Americas, New York, NY 10020

ISBN: 0-671-74991-9

First Pocket Books printing August 1995

10 9 8 7 6 5 4 3 2 1

POCKET and colophon are registered trademarks of Simon & Schuster Inc.

Cover art by Stephen Peringer

Printed in the U.S.A.

For Nate
My son, my friend, my hero.

Far, far below us the big Yukon flowing,
  Like threaded quicksilver, gleams to the eye.
                              —Robert Service

1

Belle Doyon opened her door to the creep who gunned her down. Shootings no longer surprise Americans living in the fading years of the twentieth century. In our urban battle zones, gunfire is now strictly routine. *Blam-blam-blam* and everybody hits the deck. Just ten years ago, people figured it to be a car backfiring. These days, people figure it to be bullets and get as low and as horizontal as possible. So why, for God's sake, did my friend open her door?

Belle Doyon isn't exactly your average American. For a bunch of reasons. First, because she's an Alaskan. Second, because she's a native, specifically a Koyukon Athabascan. Third, because she follows the old ways. Think of it as a lifestyle decision. What our culture terms survival skill is her daily grind. Belle can weave spruce roots into a

1

basket, run a dog team, trap a wolf, tan a hide, net a chinook, and build a shelter of snow. Which brings us to the fourth and final reason she's not your typical American. Because she lives in Tanana, population 415, a Yukon River village that is only accessible by plane, trail, or boat, depending on the season. Tanana's the kind of place where people still open their doors to strangers. Or did until some creep shot Belle.

That July day was clear in Anchorage, with a high blue sky arching over the craggy peaks of the Alaska range to the north. After parking the 4-Runner at a shooting club near my home in Eagle River, I paused for a few moments to admire Denali looming on the horizon, broad-shouldered and shawled with glaciers. Even from a distance of 125 miles, the mountain dominates the Anchorage bowl, drawing all eyes on the rare day it makes an appearance. Though I've lived in Alaska long enough to give birth to two white natives and qualify as a sourdough, I still find it hard to take my eyes off the mountain—so high, so white, and so alone. I stood in that parking lot and just stared until a pickup wheeled past, throwing up a cloud of choking dust that finally broke the spell.

I grabbed my .45-caliber Colt automatic from the passenger seat, buckled the leather belt around my hips, and settled the holster along my right thigh. Shooting hadn't held much interest for me until a few weeks earlier, when something happened that changed my life—I almost got killed. My attacker was a clever killer who had already contrived the deaths of two men and planned to make me her next victim. I showed up armed with my .45 but definitely not dangerous, since I'd tucked the automatic into the bottom of my ruck-sack along with my spare socks, sunscreen, and space blanket. As a police detective friend later pointed out, a gun's not much protection if it's out of reach. At his suggestion, I dug Max's old holster out of my bedroom closet and traded it for the smaller model I now wore. When I took my new rig over to Anchorage police headquarters for Matt Sheridan's approval, he led me downstairs to the department's test range and soon had another suggestion.

"Better start practicing, Lauren." He displayed the targets I'd been aiming for, each a two-foot square of paper with a set of rings that narrowed into a bulls-eye. "At ten feet, you barely grazed the paper." He fingered the hole in the lower right corner of the first target and then thrust the second into my hands. "From ten yards out, you missed completely."

Television makes shooting look so easy—squeeze gently and *BLAM!* For once, TV's right. Shooting is ridiculously easy. The hard part is accuracy. I'd emptied my .45 at those targets—four shots each—and had nothing to show for it except ringing ears, aching arms, and burning cheeks.

Despite the snicker at my expense, Matt Sheridan took pity on me. "Let's start with your grip. You've gotta clap that pistol between your palms."

Grip, stance, sighting, and trigger control. One month later, I had the drill down pat: palms clapped around the .45, left foot slightly forward, right arm almost straight, and left arm bending to follow the lead of the left shoulder. I worked on that at home twice a day, carefully squeezing off ten dry snaps each morning and ten more each evening, aiming for the switch plate that controlled the light in the walk-in closet in my bedroom. The purpose of my homework was to familiarize myself with the weapon and to achieve steady sighting and snapping. As I practiced at home behind closed doors, the weight of the gun in my hand graduated from unfamiliar to natural and my reflection in the mirror was no longer cause for alarm or hysterics. But the real test of my proficiency came at the shooting range. For the past month, I'd visited the range twice each week and, although I was no Dead-Eye Dick, my shooting had improved.

That July day—and every day—the potbellied attendant had a dead cigar plugged into one corner of his mouth and a half-dozen girlie magazines spread across the counter. He took his time about looking up. "How many?"

I fought the impulse to check out this month's centerfolds and instead aimed my attention at the bridge of his nose, right between his smirking pig eyes. "Three."

"Three silhouettes?"

I wondered if two words at a time were the most he could slip past that fat stogie. "Maybe next time. Three bull's-eyes for today."

He grunted, took the twenty I offered, and handed back the targets along with the change. A couple of fellows with headsets that looked like Mickey Mouse ears had commandeered the inside range, which didn't bother me. I deliberately chose to shoot outside, preferring the sea air sweeping those ranges to the sour and burnt locker-room tang clouding the air trapped inside.

After pinning up the first target at the far end of the U-shaped earthen berm, I paced off ten feet, inserted protective plugs in my ears and a fresh magazine into my .45, and then assumed the position: palms clapped, left foot forward, right arm straight, and left arm ready to bend. Trying for quickness and accuracy, I sighted carefully, held, and squeezed, all the while controlling my breathing, until I'd emptied the automatic. The Kennedy half-dollar I dug out of my jeans neatly covered the ragged hole torn in the target by my eight shots. Perfect.

The second target took more time because I sighted from ten yards out and rested between shots. At that distance, accuracy demands intense—and tiring—concentration. By the time I squeezed off my last round, sweat dampened the hair at the back of my neck but the intensity had paid off. For the first time since I'd started shooting from a distance of thirty feet, I'd achieved my goal, grouping all eight shots in an area the size of a teacup. That meant I was ready to try a new and more difficult exercise.

With the last target in place and my stance assumed, I sighted in, reminding myself to focus on the sights and let the target go blurry in the background. When the sight picture was exactly right, I started to chant in a slow cadence—"ONE for the money, TWO for the show, THREE to get ready, and FOUR to go"—firing on each numeral.

Four shots then rest, and boy did I need to rest! I was used to taking my time between rounds and so were my nerves. Four shots in quick succession hammered my central nervous system, leaving me aquiver inside and out. Needless to say, my last target was a joke. I managed to tear paper with each shot, but that group of four wouldn't fit under a roasting pan, let alone a teacup. Which was the whole point. With lives hanging in the balance, who had the luxury of taking time between shots?

I changed my chant on the final four shots. "Let the GUN do it, let the GUN do it, let the GUN do it, let the GUN do it." I got better results on the second try, but still needed at least a quiche dish to cover the group of holes left by my final rounds. At least my shooting continued to improve. After a month of practice, I'd learned that improvement was the most I could expect. For even the quickest study, proficiency took many, many hours of work.

On the way home from the shooting range, I stopped at Safeway and spent a quarter of an hour browsing through the produce department, even though the backyard garden tended by my kids provides more fresh vegetables than our family can eat. I just needed a buffer between shooting and home, a little bit of space to help me shift gears. The .45 might feel easy in my hand but that ease was part of the "new" Lauren Maxwell. She took some getting used to, especially for Jake and Jessie. Imagine waking up one day to find boring, old Mom transformed into a pistol-packing mama who biked umpteen miles to build endurance and hefted free weights to build strength. Add to Mother's new obsession the fact that her twelve-year-old son believed his failure had almost cost her life and you've got a family dynamic verging on dysfunctional. Honing my physical skills was important, but figuring out a way to resurrect Jake's self-esteem was now *the* priority. My little Jessie had done her part by wangling an invitation to join her best friend's family on a three-week visit to Disneyworld and other assorted wonders in the Lower 48. After seeing her off tomorrow, I'd be free to concentrate on helping my son. Only one question remained to be answered: *How?*

At home, I found Jake sprawled on the couch in front of the TV, deep into another installment of the new "Star Trek." Jessie scrunched at one end, impersonating the "Next Generation's" blind engineer by wearing her blue plastic headband across her eyes in imitation of the device that enables Geordi to see.

I paused in the doorway to the family room, careful to keep my gun belt out of sight behind me. "Keep that up, peanut, and you will go blind."

Jessie spared me a quick glance but Jake kept his eyes on the screen. "What's for dinner?"

I shrugged. "Good question. How does pasta sound?"

I didn't wait for their answers because pasta's always okay at our house. After dumping the .45 in a bedroom drawer, I scrounged through the kitchen and pantry until I had everything needed to concoct a fabulous garbanzo sauce for the linguine. While the water heated, I chopped onions, garlic, and tomatoes to add to the chickpeas simmering on the back burner and then stirred in some fresh rosemary from a clay pot on the back deck. Our housemate, Nina Alexeyev, created the potted herb garden when she moved in three years ago, declaring that all civilized households use fresh herbs, even those located in Alaska. Maybe when she returned from her vacation, she'd notice all the snipped herbs and finally declare victory over the dark forces of tasteless, freeze-dried convenience. Meaning me. I was counting out silverware for the table and considering excuses that might deliver even a Pyrrhic victory to the freeze-dried team when Jake croaked hoarsely from the next room.

"Mom?" And then louder. Panicked. "Mom!"

I darted into the family room to find both kids pale and wide-eyed and transfixed by a report on the six o'clock news. The screen flashed an image of a helicopter settling onto a large red cross. ". . . A life flight evacuated the shooting victim to Anchorage . . ."

The voice-over remained cool and professional

as the medicos wrenched open the door and pulled a gurney from the chopper. ". . . At five o'clock, a hospital spokesman said Miss Doyon remained in surgery . . ."

The image on the television switched back to the reporter in the studio. A photograph of my friend, John Doyon, occupied the right side of the screen. ". . . Contacted at the Anchorage headquarters of Tanana Native Corporation, the victim's brother, TNC president John Doyon, had no comment."

I shook my head, unable to take it all in, until Jessie threw herself against me and raised brimming eyes. "But, Mama, why would anyone want to hurt Belle?"

I sank to one knee and gathered her into my arms, laying my cheek against her silky hair. "I don't know why, darling."

"But we'll find out, right, Mom?" Jake turned to me with sad but stubborn eyes. "We'll find out why and who."

2

Hospitals don't bother me. My first admission came at age two after I fractured my skull falling out of the backseat of my mother's Bel Air. Four years later, I lost my tonsils. Then came a spate of emergency room visits for a couple of unstaunchable bloody noses, assorted puncture wounds requiring tetanus boosters, and a broken right arm. As a teen, I totaled my mother's Camaro in a snowstorm and also crunched my face pretty good. And in my twenties I delivered my children, both of whom seem determined to outdo their mother. Jake's been to the ER twice for stitches. Jessie had two possible poisonings—aspirin and mushrooms—and a broken wrist before she turned three. Familiarity with hospitals may not breed contempt but it does keep the anxiety level under control. Even the kids were able to decode our frequent updates on Belle's condition from Providence Hospital's patient information line.

"Stable?" Jessie puzzled that out as I tucked her in later that evening. "That means she's not getting worse, right?"

The next morning, Jake paused between gobbles of granola. "Still stable? That's good, Mom. The first couple of days decides everything, you know."

At the airport a few hours later, I managed another call while waiting for Jessie's departure. "Stable again? I wish I knew exactly what that means."

"Would you like me to connect you with the nursing station in the ICU?" The hospital operator's voice held genuine concern. "I'm sure they could explain everything."

Just then, a sleekly coifed airline attendant took up position by the door leading to the plane and one of her colleagues announced the boarding of Jessie's flight.

". . . Those passengers traveling with young children . . ."

My little girl sprang out of her chair, swung her L. L. Bean rucksack over one shoulder, and waved urgently in my direction, rising up on her toes and holding her arms wide. My heart did a somersault. I mumbled a refusal into the phone and then ran to Jessie, scooping her into my arms. "You be a good girl."

She hugged fiercely. "I will, Mama."

"Mind Megan's parents and remember to brush

11

your teeth." I gave her a squeeze and spun a slow circle. "And have a wonderful time, baby."

She reared back in my arms and leveled her wide brown eyes on mine. "I love you, Mama."

I pulled her close and pressed my lips against her ear. "I know you do, baby. And I love you, too."

Another fierce clench and then she wriggled out of my arms, shouldered her rucksack again, and trotted off to reclaim her best friend, who waited by the door to the plane. They joined hands, giggled, and threw a final kiss before disappearing through the door. As the rest of the passengers funneled toward the plane, I was left with a bad case of the airport emptiness blues and severe doubts about the wisdom of letting my eight-year-old fly anywhere without her mother in tow.

My blues descended into a deep funk on the short drive to Providence Hospital. With each of my three calls to patient information, I'd pronounced the name Belle Doyon and received an update on her condition. So I knew the television report was true, knew she'd been gravely wounded. Still, a part of me absolutely rejected that truth. The very concept that Belle Doyon could be injured seemed ludicrous. Just a few weeks earlier, I'd seen her stand fast in the face of a charging grizzly sow. I'd followed her unerring steps through willow thickets and across muskeg bogs, trusting her to find a back country cabin that maybe didn't exist. And as she settled herself on the other side of our campfire, snug in a fur robe made from pelts she'd trapped and tanned herself, I'd accepted that her connection with our great land was bred in the bone and deeper than mine could ever be. With that acceptance came something more, not quite worship and yet far greater than mere respect. What swept through me that evening with Belle Doyon was awe, an emotion that is rare indeed. Reverence tinged with fear. Wonder mingled with dread. I'd felt awe on other nights when I lay in Max's arms, marveling at the perfection of our symmetry, physical and intellectual. But the awe Belle Doyon inspired was quite different. She's the only human being I've ever known who is truly at home in the wilderness. Meaning she's just about the rarest of endangered species and one I could not bear to lose.

My denial ended when the nurse pulled open the curtain screening the door to her room in the ICU. They'd hooked her to a respirator, snaking a powder blue tube through one nostril and into her lungs, pumping in almost pure oxygen about twelve times a minute, simulating the respiration of sleep. Another machine monitored her heart rate and blood pressure from sensors taped onto her chest and cuffed around her right arm, the rhythm scrolling a jagged line across the screen while the numeric ratio flashed below. A half-dozen bags of intravenous products—blood, glucose, electrolytes—hung from a pole next to the bed, each sprouting a thin tube that led to the same square inch of horribly bruised forearm. Two matched pairs of restraints, one set for wrists and the other for ankles, held her in place and protected all of their medical marvels from her thrashing. But not one of those whirring, blinking, clicking, flashing, wheezing machines could stop her moaning.

"Oh, Belle." I tripped forward after her brother, John. He motioned me to the other side of the bed and nodded encouragement as I slipped my hand loosely around her upper arm, following his example. "Belle, it's me. Lauren."

I leaned toward her but the words caught in my throat. A white helmet of bandages swathed her head, concealing forehead and ears and eyebrows. Her eyes were mostly closed, the twitching lids mere slits in a sea of puffed and purpled flesh that had swallowed her nose and mouth and chin. A couple of bullets fired point-blank will do that to a face. I didn't want to even think about what those bullets had done to Belle Doyon's brain.

A very wise friend of mine offers two words of advice for tense moments: Get pissed. And boy, did I! Pure, holy rage flooded my veins, sweeping away the fear with a tide of certainty. "You're going to make it, Belle Doyon."

I leaned in close. "You're going to make it because you're one tough lady. And you love life. And you're too smart and too strong to ever give up. Keep fighting, Belle. Fight for all of us who love you."

A blue-coated technician with a thick, bushy beard breezed in wheeling a cart carrying spray bottles, plastic face masks, and about a zillion tubes. "Respiratory therapy. Time to go." He grinned, splitting his beard. "Gotta keep her lungs healthy so her head can heal."

Something about his all-in-a-day's-work attitude soothed my savage breast. The ICU's technology scares the hell out of most people, and rightly so. Your patient has to be in pretty bad shape to get plugged into all that machinery. And yet every day those machines manufacture miracles. Respirators keep the blood oxygenated, maintaining life at the cellular level while enforcing rest for a laboring heart. Heart monitors record minute cardiac changes, enabling quick and accurate delivery of heart-saving medicines. IVs supply a steady drip-drip-drip of magical concoctions, this one to keep the brain from swelling and that one to encourage rapid reconnection between shorted-out synapses. A quick tour of that territory by my rational scientist side left me ready to talk to John Doyon without pounding the furniture.

I followed him back to the small family waiting room and, after removing his *New York Times,* slid into a chair beside him. "Do you know what happened?"

He folded his hands into his lap and sighed. "Not really. The grandmother found her lying across the doorstep. The neurosurgeon removed two large fragments. Small caliber, maybe from a .22. One embedded at the base of her skull. The other probably did some damage."

My stomach clenched at that news. A doctor friend explained it best when he told me what happens when a small caliber bullet inside the skull lacks the oomph to break out the other side. "Imagine a brand-new tennis ball heaved through your front door. Bounces into the wall, bounces over the table, bounces against a lamp, bounces under the TV." Large caliber bullets may kill, but small caliber bullets cripple.

I laid my hand on John's shoulder. "I just don't understand how this could happen. Why would anyone in Tanana want to hurt Belle?"

Closing his eyes, John leaned his head back against the wall. "There is no one anywhere in this world with reason to hurt my sister." He shook his head slowly. "No one. I am certain of that."

With a jerk, he straightened up and pointed to a vinyl recliner in one corner of the waiting room. "I lay in that chair all through the night, remembering everything that has happened in our lives. Nothing in my memory—no person or incident, nothing!— explains what happened to Belle."

He stared at the recliner for a moment and then fixed his eyes on me. "But there is a reason, Lauren. In other places, people are shot down for no reason, but not in Tanana. And so what I think— what I fear—is that Belle might have been targeted as a stand-in for me."

Because John Doyon is not a man given to self-centered histrionics, I accepted his suspicion at face value. The Doyon siblings are the twin extremes of contemporary native culture, with Belle determined to preserve the old ways while John masters the new corporate version of tribal culture. He's the head of one of Alaska's twelve regional native corporations, which accepted forty million acres and one billion dollars to settle their land claims against the federal government. John's Tanana Native Corporation—TNC—holds title to 12.5 million acres of land and has assets in the hundreds of millions of dollars. Native or not, guys with that kind of power sometimes make deadly enemies. And frontier justice and frontier persuasion are alive and well in Alaska.

I nodded encouragement. "What's it about?"

"Oil. What else?" He tried for a smile but couldn't quite get past the worry. "Oil and real estate fuel TNC's earnings. What with the real estate bust and the S and L crisis, earnings are way down on that side of the ledger so the board has been considering raising cash by selling new oil leases."

"You can't be serious, John." Of course, I bristled. That's partly because of my job as The Wild America Society's Alaska investigator. The other part is pure instinct. We tree-huggers despise the oil industry. "TNC's already exploited every square inch of resource property. The only acreage you've got left are your subsistence lands."

"That's right. When TNC was created twenty years ago, those aboriginal lands were set aside for hunting and fishing." He shrugged. "But times change. Technology changes. Tribal needs change. And I would be derelict in my duties if I did not consider fully exploiting every asset that TNC has."

A masked woman in scrub blues poked her head

into the waiting room and gave us a quick glance before disappearing as quickly as she'd appeared. I took advantage of the distraction to collect myself, to remind myself of the great gulf of history and experience that separates white and native in Alaska. From my perspective as one of the world's haves, leaving the oil in the ground makes perfect sense. After all, look what the automobile has done to our landscape and our atmosphere. But from the have-not perspective of Alaska's natives, our environmental concerns, though legitimate, look very much like having it both ways—wealth and wilderness—at tribal expense. Plenty of whites admire Athabascans like Belle Doyon, who are determined to preserve their ancient aboriginal culture. Sometimes our admiration is so great that we forget that not every native wants to follow the old ways. We forget the Athabascans who dream of becoming doctors or movie stars or physicists or fighter pilots. Oil revenues might turn some of those dreams into reality.

Finally I nodded. "So, you're thinking about selling off mineral rights and now everybody's taking sides. But John, you've sold rights before. Nobody ever got hurt."

"The people never felt such pressure before. Or such power. Twenty years ago, Tanana was remote and game was plentiful. Now there are visitors everywhere—hiking the trails, boating the river, flying the sky—and the animals are fewer. But the people have learned much." He raised a clenched

18

fist. "About anger and shouting and power. Some talk of genocide."

I cringed at the word and his eyes lit with triumph. "See how uncomfortable that makes you? Your discomfort gives power to the one who speaks the word. So now it is said. Speaking such a word convinced the Smithsonian to return the bones of our ancestors. Successes like that breed daring in some and fear in others. Either might be cause enough to strike out. And don't forget the oil companies."

I stiffened. "Has some mangy Texan been threatening you?"

"Not really. Nothing overt, at least." John relaxed a bit, grinning at my outrage. "I thought you liked Texans. What will I tell your friend, Vannessa Larrabee? She's handling the geology on this for Fish and Game."

I snorted. "And never said a word to me. I suppose I should be honored that you both think I'm important enough to leave completely in the dark." I sighed and shook my head. "It's all so unreal. I just can't believe anybody would intentionally hurt Belle, even for oil."

John's grin faded. "Neither can the Grandmother. She refuses to take the threat seriously. In fact, she insists on returning to Tanana so she can fish. Without Belle, she'll have to do it all herself. I can't go, and my girls are too young to be of real help."

I was all set to commiserate when a vision of my son appeared in my mind's eye. Jake with the stringy muscles. Jake with the endless energy. Jake with the battered self-esteem. Q. What can one do to feel good about oneself? A. One can do unto others in need!

For the first time since hearing about Belle, my smile was genuine as I touched John Doyon's arm. "I think I have the answer to your prayers."

3

"Clean fish all summer?" My son made a gagging sound and rolled his eyes. "No way, Mom. Forget it."

Parents always hope that an appeal to their child's better nature will elicit a civilized response. Besides, I'm a legendary optimist so I bravely soldiered on, following him through the kitchen and into the family room. "Jake, think of the chance you're getting! The Grandmother is famous throughout the bush and she really needs your help."

Another roll of the eyes as he snapped on the television and settled onto the couch. I forced a bright note into my voice and came close to chirping. "You'll be living in the bush, honey! Think of what she'll teach you!"

His eyes steadied on the TV screen, but a smirk

marred his handsome face. "Star Trek's" new generation was at it again. "Think of the slimey fish guts, Mom. And the swarms of mosquitoes."

I positioned myself in front of the television, forcing Jake to look at me. And I jettisoned the appeal to his better nature and moved straight on to bribery. "Think of that mountain bike you've been whining about. Why should I even consider getting it for a kid with this kind of attitude?"

His cheeks reddened and he thrust out his chin. "Why should I waste my summer busting my butt for some old lady I don't even know?"

Fists clenched, I took a step toward him. The movement had nothing to do with playacting and everything to do with fury. How could a child of mine, a child of Max's, be so callous? Anger released the whip in my tongue. "Why, Jake? I'll tell you why."

I thrust out an index finger and jabbed it in his direction. "Because that old lady is the grandmother of Belle and John Doyon."

I added a finger and jabbed again. "Because when your dad's plane went down, John Doyon put every aircraft TNC owns into the air to search for him."

I raised a third finger and jabbed again. "Because when your dad's plane went down, Belle Doyon harnessed up her dog team to search for him."

Jake's eyes teared and a tremble passed over his stubborn chin, but I wouldn't relent. "Because we owe them. Because they're our friends. Because your father would do it. Because it's the right thing to do."

Grief and shame twisted my son's face into an ugly knot as the tears spilled over. He had time for one ragged inhalation before the storm broke over him, a squall of choked sobs and anguished moans and endless tears that curled him against the cushions of the couch.

My anger receded, leaving me weak-kneed and ashamed of my bullying. Twelve is such an awkward age—too old for innocence but too young for reality. And maybe mentioning Max wasn't quite fair. Jake had been old enough to have specific and detailed memories of his warm and loving father. Given his personality, my son will never be casual about his loss or become resigned to it.

I knelt beside him and gently laid a hand on his heaving back, rubbing slow circles and murmuring soothing hushabyes. My own eyes welled with tears of longing tinged with anger. At times, I almost hated Max for dying. Most often those times occurred when Jake needed more than I could give. I'm not sure if every boy absolutely needs a father, but I'm certain that my son's life would unfold more smoothly if his dad were around to help. Even Jake's friendship with a terrific man named Travis MacDonald couldn't come close to making up for the loss of his father. Theirs had been a very unusual bond, one forged from the moment of Jake's birth when Max cradled the startled newborn, introduced himself, and then wished his son a happy birthday. When some tumult in Jake's life left me feeling inadequate, I longed for Max and his magical ability to make everything all better for all of us.

In time, Jake's shudders and sobs subsided, giving way to trembling and sniffing before he finally quieted. For a moment, he lay still. Then he stretched out full-length and heaved himself onto his back, eyes still squeezed tight. When he opened his eyes, they quickly filled with concern. "Mom? Are you crying?"

I brushed the thick bangs off his forehead. "Just a little."

He frowned. "But why?"

I sighed. "Because I made you cry. I'm sorry about that. And because I miss your dad. He was so much better with you kids."

"Yeah, but you do okay." At my raised eyebrow, a familiar teasing light flashed into his eyes. "If I said you were better than Dad you'd know I was lying. But you *are* doing okay."

"Thanks for the vote of confidence." I sat back on my heels, preparing to disengage. "So. What have you decided about helping the Grandmother in fish camp?"

"I'll go." He reached out and grabbed my hand. "But please, can I have that mountain bike? Can I take it with me? Please?"

One of Jake's great charms is his willingness to let bygones be bygones and get on with it. Life's little disasters don't phase him. He makes the best of things without being a martyr. He's not a grudge holder and his enthusiasm for life knows no bounds. All of which means he's a real asset in the bush and on the trail. All of that also explains why I'm a complete sucker for him.

I leaned in to plant a kiss on his forehead. For once, he didn't squirm away. That's because he knows how to play his mother. "Please, Mom?"

"You can have the mountain bike." I stood up and moved toward the door. "If you promise to wear your helmet."

"Aaawww, Mom." I stopped and looked back at him over my shoulder. A grin split his face. "Just kidding." He zapped the TV on with the remote control and settled himself against the couch. "These are the voyages of Jake Maxwell. His summertime mission is to explore new trails, to end salmon's life, to boldly go where only natives have gone before."

On that note, I left my Trekkie and went into my bedroom to give John Doyon the good news. I phoned the hospital but he wasn't in the ICU's family waiting room. The receptionist at TNC headquarters told me he was expected but hadn't yet arrived. I left a message and then decided to clean my gun while waiting for his call.

Like everything else about my gunnery, cleaning the .45 was a private ritual. I kept a supply of rags, a brush, and bottles of solvent and oil under the sink in my bathroom and usually did the job behind a double set of closed doors. Not that I was ashamed of my new avocation. In fact, I took some pride in my diligent practice, particularly after a good set of drills at the shooting range. So the gun wasn't the problem. The problem was in my head.

I cut a small square of clean cloth and used a ramrod to insert the patch into the bore, swabbing out the barrel of the automatic. In the years we shared, Max must have cleaned the .45 many times, yet I had no memory of it. My husband was no wild-eyed gun nut but having the weapon around still bothered me. He must have sensed my unease because he handled the thing very discreetly, holstering it without comment on trips in the bush and leaving it out of sight at home.

I dipped the small bristle brush in G. I. solvent and scrubbed the bore. After Jake's birth, safety became a major concern. One afternoon I tuned in a talk show and heard a parade of grieving parents recount the accidental home shootings that had cost them a child. That show sent me flying for the bedroom closet to make sure Max's damned gun was safely out of reach. When I couldn't find it, I called him at the veterinary clinic, frantic to locate the .45 before my son could kill himself.

As usual, Max approached the problem reasonably. "Can't it wait till I get home, Lauren? After all, he's only six months old."

As so often happened in those postpartum days, the reasonable approach left me feeling quite unreasonable. "No. We might forget. I want to deal with it now because I'm thinking about it now."

By that time in our parenthood, Max had

learned to humor my sudden fits. "It's locked in a metal strongbox that I keep in the closet. My side, top shelf, way in the back."

That information immediately posed a new problem. "Locked? Where's the key?"

His sigh held a trace of amusement. He knew what was coming. "On my key ring."

My voice sharpened. "Why don't I have a key?"

He could have met my challenge with a rude rejoinder. For example: Because you've never given a damn about the gun before today! Instead, experience had taught Max a better way of handling his life partner. "Why don't I get you one on my way home? We'll take the strongbox down and you tell me whether it's really secure."

Aretha Franklin said it best: "R-E-S-P-E-C-T. Find out what it means to me." Having had my concern greeted respectfully, I was ready to compromise. "Thanks, Max. You're a really great guy." He certainly was. Better than I deserved.

I left the .45's barrel wet, soaked another patch with solvent, and wiped the ramp, bolt face, and slide rails free of powder residue. The only legitimate complaint I had about my husband was the love of risk that eventually cost us his life. Put simply, Max was an adrenaline junkie. He liked to do hard and dangerous things. He said that increasing the risk increased the fun. He wasn't really a daredevil, although I called him that a time or two. I didn't understand him then. I really thought then that my husband had a death wish.

Drying the barrel took two patches and I used a third to oil the gun inside and out. I didn't really understand Max's need to push life to the farthest edge, to lean over that precipice and risk it all. I didn't understand because I hadn't been there. But recently two things happened that changed all that: I stood my ground at a grizzly's charge and later managed to keep my cool while a captive of my would-be murderer. After those incidents, the air smelled sweeter, the sun shone brighter, my heart beat stronger, and I finally understood the man who'd been my husband. Now that I've been there, I want to go back. That's the problem in my head and the reason I'm so discreet with the .45.

After tightening all screws, I put the gun back in the locked box and stowed it on the shelf in my closet. No longer Max's side but still the same security system. Trust him to do it right. I had trusted him in everything. That's why I married him and why I'll never stop missing him.

I dashed across my bedroom when the phone rang and I picked up on the first ring. John Doyon's secretary put me right through to her boss. "Everything's set on my end. Jake was looking for something interesting to do this summer."

John's voice held a note of caution. "You may want to reconsider in light of some new information."

I sank onto the bed. "What new information?"

"The Grandmother tells me somebody's been leaving skinned wolves on her doorstep. The first about a month ago and then another one last week."

Before I could ask the obvious question, John answered it as best he could. "I'm not sure what those skinned wolves mean, Lauren, but I'm certain it can't be good."

4

Those wolf pelts changed everything. For me, at least. But Jake didn't see it my way. At the potential for danger and hint of mystery, my son's interest and enthusiasm for fish camp soared. And he proceeded to use my own best arguments against me.

"It's the right thing to do. You said so, Mom." He straightened his thin shoulders, bringing his eyes almost level with mine. "They're our friends. We owe them. And Dad would want us to."

Smart-ass kid certainly had my number. No way could I be such an obvious hypocrite. And though I'll admit to an interest in preserving my own self-esteem, I'll also lay claim to living up to my son's expectations. Jake thinks of me as one of the good guys. Do the right thing was my operative philosophy long before Spike Lee filmed his movie. Having hammered home that phrase ad nauseam, I certainly couldn't abandon the belief at the first sign of adversity. Maybe that's the way most people find the courage of their convictions. I know it worked for me.

"You're right, Jake." I collared him with one arm, pulling him close. "Thanks for reminding me."

"No problem, Mom." He tried for casual but my praise had touched off a blaze of pride that left his eyes gleaming. "So, when do we leave?"

"I'll need some time to square things away at work." I cocked my head and mentally ran through my schedule. "Probably day after tomorrow. We'll catch a late flight."

He gave me his most winning grin. "Cool. I'll go check out my gear."

After Jake trotted off in search of his camping gear, I moved into the kitchen to build a couple of pizzas. He'd put in a special request for the meal and even offered to make the crust. As he'd promised, I located the dough on top of the refrigerator, well risen and poofing against the plastic wrap that covered the metal bowl. Jake's crusts are better than mine because he sets the timer for ten minutes and then kneads to the very last second. Too bad he doesn't show the same fanaticism about cleaning up.

I drew a sink full of hot water, added a healthy squirt of dish liquid, and set about tidying his mess. Were all kids such a mass of contradictions, with each endearing trait inextricably entwined with an infuriating one? So often Jake left me feeling absolutely helpless. A couple of years ago, he sneaked out of the house with a big fishing knife and managed to cut his thumb down to the bone. In the face of my furious demand for an explanation, he raised huge teary eyes to me. "I was playing pretend, Mom. I just wanted to be a hero."

My heart clenched at the memory as I wiped the last scatter of flour from the counter. My Jake wanted to be a hero. That's what had me worried. Everybody needs a chance to stretch themselves and test their limits, kids included. But what had been done to Belle was not pretend. If the whole Doyon family was in danger, I didn't want my son in the middle of it. Not without me at his side.

The food processor took mere seconds to chew up a ball of mozzarella and a wedge of Parmesan. I dumped both grated cheeses into a bowl and blended by hand. Alaska may be immense but just about each of her 591,000 square miles can be considered at risk for environmental disaster. Which is a boon for the job security and travel allowance of the resident investigator of the Wild America Society. Meaning me. What with the climate changing, population booming, and a new generation of developers eager to rape the land, travel to any corner of the state can be justified on the basis of looming ecological crisis. In the Koyukon region alone, I had a good half-dozen problems to choose from.

I pulled the paper from four inches of pepperoni and then oh-so-carefully sliced off enough to top one pizza. What I needed was a problem that would keep me in the bush as long as the Grandmother needed Jake's assistance. Meaning at least a couple of weeks. That eliminated a simple fact-finding trip or press-the-flesh PR blitz. Both types of visits lasted a few days at most. And it was too late in the season to organize a wilderness expedition for a bunch of the Wild America's managerial honchos and deep-pocket donors from the Lower 48. That type of crowd usually had plans for August that involved yachting, islands, or races, preferably all three. Roughing it in mosquito heaven had little appeal on such short notice.

After slicking a dollop of olive oil across my palms and separating the dough into two balls, I shaped and stretched each ball to fit a circular fourteen-inch pan. Having eliminated as possibilities all the easy and/or fun stuff, what remained was just work. Fieldwork, to be exact. Also known as hard work because of the minute observation, precise counting, detailed note taking, and careful sketching that research in the field entails. If reading your latest scholarly paper to an international conference is biology's heaven, then the sunrise to sunset minutiae of fieldwork is biology's hell. Imagine spending weeks mucking around in a primitive camp, eating tasteless prepackaged glop, sleeping on the ground, bathing in a bucket, and peeing in a hole, only to conclude upon returning to the world that your work adds up to zilch in terms of science. (To be honest, that sounds like my kind of heaven, but then Alaska investigator for the

Wild America Society is hardly mainstream science.) Ever wonder why you read so often about faked research? The dubious nature of fieldwork is a major part of the answer.

I spooned out the tomato sauce, spread the blended cheeses, artfully topped one pie with pepperoni, and slid both pans into the oven, preheated to 450 degrees. Coming up with a suitable project near Tanana proved to be a cinch. In fact, I came up with two: surveying the Nowitna River's resident sheefish population and cataloging the valley's remnant Beringian era steppe vegetation. Both jobs fell under the category of inventory. Biologically speaking, we're still in the early stages of figuring out exactly what this planet contains. With the big time extinctions now under way, we're losing species we haven't even named. The Nowitna's steppe vegetation has been around since Alaska and Asia were connected by a land bridge known as Beringia about 36,000 years ago, and the river's resident sheefish are exceedingly rare, with only three known populations on earth. To my mind, the longevity of one species and rarity of the other provided ample justification for fieldwork. Their location near the Grandmother's fish camp didn't hurt, either.

When the tops of the pizzas started to brown, I pulled the pans from the oven and slid the pies onto racks to cool. For once, adjusting my work schedule to my personal needs wouldn't require too much juggling. Just last week I'd signed, sealed, and shipped to my boss in Washington a comprehensive report detailing the many scientific reasons for prohibiting oil exploration within the Arctic National Wildlife Refuge. Boyce Reade and his underlings in the Lower 48 believe that keeping the drill rigs out of that prime caribou habitat is the Wild America Society's number-one job in Alaska. From my in-state point of view, ANWR was just one of too damn many places that needed protection.

Ever so gently, I laid two squares of paper towel across the top of the pepperoni pizza and, in the fashion of every truly nineties chef, sopped up all the excess oil. Nobody could really complain if I farmed out the impact study for the proposed Paint River fish ladder. After all, my near-fatal encounters with a maddened grizzly and a murderous woman had occurred within hollering distance of the Paint, and the psychic wounds from those adventures had barely scabbed over. No way I'd be persuaded to go tramping through that country again any time soon. Given ten days' time and average abilities, any fish biologist could do a competent job down there. I'd have one hired by the end of the day tomorrow.

After pouring soda for Jake and jug red for myself, I doled out four triangles of pizza. With the ANWR study complete and the Paint River impact farmed out, the only pressing matter left on my desk was a long-scheduled seminar for some tourists visiting the oil spill area of Prince William Sound. Ecotourists are my kind of vacationers. Forget destinations like Vegas and Orlando. These folks take it easy by climbing Mount Shasta or rafting the Colorado or cycling the Oregon coast. In my seminar, they're expected to master the latest techniques for rescuing oiled critters so they could form first-response teams in their own localities. They are the kind of committed do-gooders who volunteer and who vote, write checks, and write letters. People of influence, in other words, and the one item on my work agenda that could not be postponed or farmed out. That seminar in Valdez was a must. Fortunately, I'd have a couple of days first to get my son settled with the Grandmother. And I wouldn't be gone long. A day at most.

"It's pizza time," I sang out while carrying our plates across the kitchen, and then laid them on facing mats. Without place settings for Jessie and Nina, the wooden table looked bare, almost lonely, and the house suddenly seemed too quiet. "Jake? Dinner!"

No answer. From that silence came a spurt of panic with more than enough zing to carry me out of the kitchen and up the stairs. First time something really bad happens, you can't believe it. Given a while to digest the horror, you start expecting the worst. My hand trembled as it twisted Jake's doorknob.

He bent over the circle of high intensity light pooled on his desk, nodding his head in time to the music plugged into his ears, eyes intent on the blade of the Swiss Army knife that his fingers gently worked against the sharpening stone.

I leaned against the door, weak-kneed and light-headed as the adrenaline rush tapered off. Jake didn't notice me right away so I had a few seconds to study the tableaux. A boy taking care of his gear. A boy who just wanted to be a hero. A boy so like his father that it scared me. Suddenly even a day apart seemed way too long.

5

Two days later, Jake and I climbed into one of John Doyon's TNC planes for the flight to Tanana. Turned out we weren't the only ones thumbing a ride. Exactly 253 Athabascan ancestors were also on board, neatly packed inside 118 sturdy cardboard boxes. A Smithsonian Institution anthropologist had dug up their graves and carted their bones to Washington about sixty years earlier. Now after some major hassling that finally ended with an act of Congress, the ancestors were coming home for good.

Once we were airborne I studied the ground whizzing by below, but Jake kept turning around to survey the boxes stowed in the cargo space behind our seats. "Kind of creepy, don't you think?"

"Just bones, sweetie." I grinned and broke into song. "Dem bones, dem bones, dem dry bones."

"Not the bones." He rolled his eyes. "I mean the way some guy just dug 'em up and took 'em, you know? I mean, Indiana Jones didn't do stuff like that. He never took anybody's bones. Old statues, medallions, jewels—that's the kind of stuff he took."

I cocked an eyebrow. "That kind of stuff is also known as the loot. And statues, medallions, and jewels are archaeology." I jerked a thumb in the direction of the Smithsonian's loot. "Bones are anthropology. By the time the Americans got into the act, the good stuff was already gone. Only thing left to loot was bones." I couldn't resist another warble. "Dem bones, dem bones, dem dry bones."

After hearing those definitions, Jake's brow creased and he sat back with his thinking face on. I returned to my aerial survey, charting our progress against my mental map. In a few minutes, the Anchorage basin would fall away behind as the plane threaded through a low spot on the Alaska Range, between Denali to the west and Mount Hayes to the east. To me, the interior begins at Broad Pass, because from there all waters flow to the Yukon, the mighty river that is the heart and soul and lifeblood of the Alaskan bush.

Jake's touch on my arm drew my attention from the window. "Remember at the end of the first movie how those guys nailed the Ark of the Covenant into a box marked Top Secret?"

Indiana Jones again. I nodded. Jake got the movie for Christmas one year, and we've watched it so often that I have Karen Allen's best lines down by heart.

He leaned across the narrow aisle. "Remember how it ends with the box stuck on a shelf in this huge warehouse filled with a bazillion other boxes marked Top Secret? Do you think that happens for real? Important stuff getting forgotten?"

Again I nodded. "Yes to both questions, kiddo. In fact, it happened with these bones. One thing holding up their return was the fact that nobody had bothered to look at them for 60 years. The museum got interested only when the village asked for them back. They've been waiting for a couple of years."

"I'll bet they're pissed." A beatific smile spread across his face as he again settled into his seat. Like all adolescents, my son is charmed by the idea of strong, negative emotions. "I'll bet everybody in Tanana's *really* pissed."

Jake's guess turned out to be just about right. After clearing the mountains, the plane steadied for an hour over the interior lowlands, a thick carpet of spruce carved by meandering streams and dotted with muskeg bogs, before finally swooping low over the wide, gleaming Yukon on the final approach to Tanana. The whole village had gathered at the airfield to pay homage to the ancestors, and Jake and I stepped out of the plane to face a silent circle of Athabascans. Although the *Dene* are legendary for shirt-off-their-back hospitality, they aren't chumps. Who could blame them if our arrival pushed the limits of their graciousness? Thank God, I'd left my automatic in my backpack.

Snagging Jake's elbow, I edged down the length of the plane, all the while studying the crowd and wondering which steely pair of eyes belonged to Belle Doyon's attacker. Elders held the first rank on the tarmac, the old men solemn-eyed under the brims of their ball caps while the old women hugged themselves inside their zippered sweat-shirts. The youngest children stood close by their mothers and while a couple danced from foot to foot, even those toddlers remained quiet. Here and there stood small knots of adolescents, the teenage girls hovering in close while the teenage boys positioned themselves on the far edge of the crowd. The mere scattering of men of middle years meant that the annual summer migration of the able-bodied was under way, with sons and fathers leaving the village to earn a seasonal paycheck on a crew fighting fires or building roads. Today even a subsistence lifestyle requires cash for gasoline and spare parts.

Much to my relief, the villagers soon lost interest in us, especially when two young fellows with all-terrain vehicles showed up, each ATV towing a high-sided wagon and both very much in need of new mufflers. A youngish woman who'd made a point of glaring at us stepped forward and started giving orders. She organized the crowd with such energy that the single traditional braid hanging down her back swung to and fro, slapping her sturdy shoulders. In minutes, she'd formed the villagers into two lines to unload the plane. The boxes passed from hand to hand, all 118 of them traveling down a human chain that stretched from aircraft to ATV, a community chain of elders and adolescents and mothers with tiptoeing children who gently cradled their 253 unknown ancestors.

Inside my head, I heard the refrain of the song I'd sung earlier—dem bones, dem bones, dem dry bones—and knew shame as intense as any I'd ever felt. Cynicism is easy, respect is hard. And yet for these people of Tanana, whose subsistence lifestyle is defined as mere existence, respect came as naturally as breathing. Since their first meeting with members of our majority culture, the Athabascans have been decimated by disease, devalued by racism, and debased by alcohol, and yet the *Dene* have survived. They have not thrived and they have not prospered, but the *Dene* have endured our worst and survived.

A tiny sound came from the boy beside me, drawing my eyes. Jake pressed his lips together to still their trembling but did nothing to hide the two glistening tracks left by his tears. He didn't meet my eyes, focusing instead on the sad work of the villagers.

I swung an arm around my son's shoulders and gave him a quick squeeze, my own shame dissolved by the pride I took in him. His eyes never wavered, staying steady as the work of the sorrowful community wound down, unflinching as the final boxes moved toward the ATVs, leaving empty hands behind. When the last of the cartons were piled into the high-sided wagons, the ATV drivers gently gunned their engines and moved off down the tarmac. One by one, the people of Tanana fell into step behind, forming a hushed procession that moved off at a slow pace.

As their numbers dwindled, the villagers' interest in us revived, particularly that of the bossy woman with the single braid. She hovered around the fringes of the crowd, exchanging hushed words with one person or another, but seeming more interested in watching us than talking to anyone. The naked hostility in her dark eyes didn't surprise me. This us-and-them world generates a lot of anger by forever choosing up sides and making the losers pay big time. Even a people as generous and hospitable as the *Dene* have their share of haters. For me, the important question was how nasty this one would be.

I had the answer almost immediately. Shoulders squared and chin held high, she stalked toward us and asked a blunt and imperious question of her own. "Why are you coming here? Tourists aren't needed now."

"We're not tourists." Another quick squeeze of Jake's shoulders and then I dropped my arm and presented my antagonist with a gesture as old as time, prominently displaying my unarmed hands. I also smiled. "We're guests."

Apparently she read both gesture and smile as mockery. Her eyes snapped and she hissed her next question. "Whose guest?"

I paused long enough to breathe in deeply and

43

exhale slowly, savoring the rich, earthy scent of the river. No good purpose would be served by letting the woman tick me off. And losing my temper wouldn't set much of an example for Jake, either. I caught his eye and gave him a quick nod before turning back to Tanana's resident witch. "Why don't you tell us who you are first?"

Our confrontation had attracted a small circle of stragglers, one of whom answered my question. "That's Eleanor Demissov. From the village council."

The information certainly sharpened the focus, providing an essential context for her hostility. A militant. One with power. Just then I didn't feel the need to make another native enemy for the Wild America Society. My goal was to transform from one of her stereotypes into another less threatening. From Ugly American into Clumsy-but-Harmless American.

I thrust a hand at her. "Lauren Maxwell."

She ignored my hand, and her eyes drifted to my son. I waved a hand to include him in my greeting. "And this is my son, Jake. I'm sure you know our hostess. Sarah Doyon?"

That set the onlookers to murmuring among themselves. Eleanor Demissov narrowed her dark eyes. "You come to the Grandmother?"

I tried for a bright tone of voice. "You *do* know her!" Again I waved a hand at my son, throwing in a wide smile this time. "Jake's here to give her a hand in fish camp. And I'm here to help *him* get settled."

Like a punch-drunk fighter I was saved by the bell. Make that bells, as in steeple. One after another, the bells of Tanana's mission churches started to ring, pealing out a mournful salute to the ancestors. The brass chorale sent the last of the villagers off at a trot. Eleanor Demissov remained behind just long enough to issue an order. "Now is the burial. Tonight the potlatch. The Grandmother comes. You do not."

Miss a genuine potlatch? No chance. Still, it wouldn't do to say so. Fighting down the temptation to confess myself a complete party animal, I stayed in character, laying a hand on my breastbone and opening my eyes wide. "Of course not. We wouldn't *dream* of intruding."

That must have satisfied her. Without another word, Eleanor Demissov turned and walked away. When she was safely out of hearing range, Jake let his breath out in a huff. "Boy, is she something! I didn't like her, Mom."

"No reason why you should." I gave him one of those locker-room fanny slaps you see all the time in the NBA. The whole village would attend the potlatch. Including Belle's attacker. "Not to worry, sweetie. I'm sure everyone else will be friendly."

He accepted that with a nod and then threw me a playful grin. "You were pretty gross yourself." He moved into falsetto. "Soooo good to see you. Of course, dahhling." He snorted with disgust. "What a faker!"

Without answering, I hefted my bag and headed down the tarmac toward the village. Jake slung his backpack to his shoulders, settled the frame on his hips, and followed. "No offense, Mom. And I did like the last thing you said. About not intruding? For once, maybe we should just leave them alone."

That settled it. I'd wanted to attend an authentic potlatch for years, but Jake wanted to leave them alone. And so we would.

6

Sarah Doyon won my son's undying devotion with four simple words: "You drive the boat."

We spent the morning after the ancestors' potlatch packing gear for the move downriver to fish camp. Compared to many contemporary Athabascans, the Grandmother traveled light, leaving behind the trappings of modern bush living—television, microwave oven, and VCR. Still, Jake trudged off with boxes loaded with staples like pilot bread, Jell-O, Spam, canned mandarin oranges, and Hills Brothers coffee. I tripped after him, arms laden with fish nets reeking of last year's catch. The Grandmother came last, carrying two small bags and one huge radio. Nothing short of disaster prevents her from tuning in Tundra Topics each night.

Down by the river I dropped the nets and filled

my lungs with sweeter Yukon air. The current sent the engine-weighted sterns of about a dozen boats swinging downstream, leaving bows tugging against buoys. Experienced boaters learn to read each ripple and wave of the river because glacial powders leave the water opaque, almost milky. Born in British Columbia, just 15 miles from the Pacific, the Yukon swings a great arc north and west for 2,300 miles before emptying into the Bering Sea at Norton Sound. At breakup, the river's flow can reach ten miles an hour and two hundred thousand cubic feet per second, sweeping hundreds of millions of tons of ice down to the sea. Timber also floats in the torrent, entire trees that plunge into the river after raging waters cave in banks. A thousand miles downstream, that wood becomes the river's gift to Eskimos who have relied on the Yukon for fuel for untold centuries, a people of the barren tundra whose ancestors never saw a living tree.

The Grandmother pointed out a battered aluminum sled sporting a twenty-five-horsepower outboard before taking a seat on the edge of beached raft in need of another fifty-gallon oil can float. Jake wrestled the boat to shore and then did the grunt work. I followed Sarah Doyon's lead and swallowed the urge to give directions. Turned out my son had more common sense than I'd ever given him a chance to display. To keep our sleeping bags dry, he came up with a couple of plastic garbage pail liners. For added protection, he stowed the plastic bags under the shallow deck of the bow. The food boxes he piled along the keel and secured tightly with bungee cords. The diciest part of loading proved to be finding a secure spot for a cylinder of natural gas for the Grandmother's cookstove. Jake tried several alternatives before deciding to pillow the gas on his backpack, which he then strapped to the floor of the boat. When he'd finished with the gas, he propped his hands on his hips and spent a few minutes studying his handiwork before turning around to toss a question to the Grandmother. "You think that'll be okay?"

Sarah Doyon nodded as she got to her feet, knotting the ends of a bright head scarf under her chin and saying the magic words. "You drive the boat."

A Christmas morning grin spread across Jake's face. He hustled us into our life jackets and then hustled us into the sled. I had to fiddle with my life jacket to get it over the gun on my hip. Jake didn't seem to notice, but the Grandmother certainly did. I ignored the question in her eyes.

The Grandmother didn't seem concerned when the outboard sputtered to life and then quickly died each time my son yanked the starter cord. She sat in the bow, her heavily lined face placid inside her scarf of red roses as she watched the frantic efforts of a pair of swallows whose nest had come to the attention of a circling hawk.

I resisted the urge to turn around but, from my position amidships, easily overheard the frantic efforts and quiet commentary of my son.

"Gas line attached?" A small movement rocked the boat. "Check!"

"Choke on?" A definite click. "Check!"

"Engine primed?" A couple of liquid squeezes. "Check!"

"Throttle in neutral?" The tiniest pause. "Nope! Can't start her up when she's in gear."

Good thing! Talk about common sense. Lately that's something most engineers seem to lack. Ever wonder why only one of the planet's car manufacturers has seen fit to rig headlights to turn off automatically when the engine does?

Behind me, Jake grunted with the effort of pulling the outboard's starter. This time the engine hardly sputtered before settling into a high-pitched whine that drowned my musings about the design defects of modern manufacturing. The boat moved forward with a small but definite jerk, and suddenly I had plenty of other things to worry about.

In late summer, the Yukon possesses a stately flow that whispers by wide sandbars and gurgles through a maze of twisting passages. Jake piloted the boat with more care than skill, maintaining a speed that hardly beat the current. I didn't complain and neither did the Grandmother. Although I didn't know her well, I sensed an eagerness building as we traveled downriver. In every year of her long life, Sarah Doyon had made this trip, a pilgrimage almost, one fraught with great meaning and huge consequences. In subsistence living, a good summer lays the foundation for a good winter. Getting a moose in autumn is nice, but getting the fish in summer is essential. Without fish there is no survival.

A quiet kind of gaiety transformed the Grandmother as we traveled downstream. She trailed a hand in the water and sprinkled a few drops on her withered cheeks. Later, she lifted her face to the sun and sniffed the air. When a boat heading upriver whizzed by, she threw up an exuberant hand to wave. Further on, a fish wheel scooped a fat salmon from the water and she laughed out loud. Around another bend she played tour guide, pointing out the high bluffs of frozen silt on the south shore. "The boneyards. Many animals from distant time."

I smiled and nodded and turned to Jake to repeat the information and add some of my own. "Also known as the Palisades. Some of the finds there date back to the Ice Age. Just like the plants I'll be studying at Nowitna."

Jake allowed himself a quick glance. "Cool." He finger combed wind-whipped hair with one hand as his eyes returned to the river ahead. "How much farther d'you think?"

The Grandmother sang out in reply. "Not far."

No more than a mile downstream, in fact. The Doyons had built their fish camp on a bench on the sunnier northern shore. In a cleared space amid towering spruce, three cabins ranged at angles around the drying racks. The smallest cabin featured a basketball hoop and the largest had glass in the window frames. An enormous fish wheel teetered on the edge of the bench, held in place by a rope securely tied to a nearby tree.

Jake gave the outboard the gas, running the sled onto the narrow beach. "Home sweet fish camp." He vaulted out of the boat and trotted forward to offer a smile and an arm to the Grandmother. "Looks pretty cool."

Indeed it did. I carried a load of boxes from the beach and then paused to admire the view. The afternoon sun sprinkled diamonds across the platinum river and mirrored the shaggy spruce lining both shores. The land to the south rose in stages, first climbing the rounded green humps of the Kuskokwim Mountains and then scaling the jagged ice peaks of the Alaska Range. A dazzling sky canopied all, and my chest ached with pleasure at such beauty.

Our arrival didn't go unnoticed. The first raven showed up before the Grandmother had time to throw open the windows of the large cabin. He circled over the fish camp, slowly flapping his glossy black wings, then chose a front-row spruce as his perch and croaked a hoarse greeting. Soon a second bird appeared and then a third, both taking their time about choosing just the right branch from which to watch the show. Raven isn't shy and seldom hurries. He is the clown of the boreal forest, the wittiest denizen of the Alaskan bush, and perhaps the cleverest of the many clever species that inhabit the Koyukon country. Raven lets others do his hunting, especially humans and wolves, and deigns to feast upon their leftovers, an act of utter noblesse oblige. To Westerners raven's a pest, but to natives he's a god. The Creator, in fact.

The Grandmother finally wrestled the window open and leaned out, arms resting on the wood sill as she addressed our visitors. *"Tseek'aal,* bring us luck with the fish!"

Ggaakk-ggaakk-ggaakk.

The raven's cries caught Jake's attention as he climbed up from the beach, balancing the cylinder of gas across his shoulders. He swung the tank off his back and set it beside the cottage. "What did you call him?"

"Tseek'aal." A wide smile folded the Grandmother's cheeks into a maze of wrinkles. "Old grandfather. He gives luck."

Jake cocked his head to study the circle of ravens. "How come?"

"Raven gives luck because he built Alaska." She raised a clawed hand and dug the air. "Raven dug the river with his foot."

Jake shaded his eyes against the afternoon sun. "But ravens are such scavengers." He looked at the Grandmother and shrugged. "No offense or anything, but sometimes they're a real pain."

"That is so." She threw her arms wide to embrace both river and mountains. "Yet Raven built Alaska. And from distant time, raven has helped the *Dene* many times."

"Tell us, please." I stepped forward, eager to hear a tale from the Grandmother. Athabascans have a strong oral tradition, one that both describes and preserves their tribal history and knowledge of the natural world. "Jake only knows Raven's mischief."

After a moment's hesitation, she nodded, then ducked back into the cabin to remove her head scarf before coming outside. The Grandmother chose a sunny spot on the woodpile for her seat, tilting her face to catch the warm rays. I settled onto the ground in front of her and motioned Jake to join me. The quiet of the bush settled over us, broken only by the buzz of an insect, the whispered hush of the river's flow, and the Grandmother's quiet voice.

"One morning toward winter, the sun did not rise. Seeing fear in the *Dene,* Raven asked why and learned a rich man took both the sun and the moon. So Raven promised to get them back."

Alerted by Jake's intake of breath, I laid a hand on his arm and gave him a sharp squeeze. His breath whooshed out in a loud sigh, but at least he didn't speak. The Grandmother lowered her face and finally addressed us directly.

"Raven saw the rich man's daughter drinking from a creek so he turned himself into a little tuft of moss and was drunk down. Soon a child was born."

Again the Grandmother paused but this time Jake made no move to speak. I patted his arm and then let my hand fall away.

"The child wanted to play with the sun and the moon. Only the moon, said the rich man, and so it was. But after the moon, the child still wanted the sun. Again and again and again, the child asks to play with the sun."

No matter the culture, kids are still kids. And as the Grandmother's story illustrates, all around the world the adults usually cave in.

"The rich man closed up his house tight and let the child play. Time and again, the boy threw up the sun, each time a little closer to the smoke hole in the peak of the roof. Closer and closer until out went the sun and out went the moon. Then the child became Raven and followed the sun and the moon."

Jake kept quiet, resisting the universal adolescent urge to step on the punch line. As for myself, I resisted the universal parental urge to point out the obvious moral.

If the Grandmother found our reticence unusual for non-natives, she didn't mention it. She just smiled. "So from distant time until today, the *Dene* don't mind Raven's tricks because his tricks saved the sun and the moon."

We sat silently for a few minutes. Then two of the watching ravens took flight, swooping toward the boat on the beach below. Jake bounced to his feet. "Maybe they aren't so bad, but I better get down there, just in case."

When his head dropped from sight, the Grandmother turned sharp eyes on me. "Lauren Maxwell, why do you wear that gun?"

I resisted the urge to lower my eyes. Elder or no, I refused to let her desire to minimize the attack on Belle put us all in danger. I patted the handle of the automatic. "Just in case I run into any bad wolves."

She gave me a hard stare and I stared right back. Finally she hhmmpphhed, and I knew I'd won. "What do you know about those wolves, Grandmother?"

She shook her head. "Nothing. I know nothing."

Still I stared.

And then she sighed. "I have those wolves. Maybe their skins say something."

7

Sometimes science gives me the chills. That's what happened when I took one of the wolf pelts to a researcher I knew at the Fairbanks campus of the University of Alaska and asked what could be learned by studying the hide.

Marisa Dorn snorted and rolled her eyes. "Plenty." She ran a hand over fur left stiff by the dried blood of the animal's crude skinning. "Why don't you narrow the field by telling me what specifically you'd like to know?"

I brushed a strand of hair out of my eyes and weighed the possibilities. To be honest, my purpose was vague. I didn't really understand the significance of the wolf pelts that had been left at Belle Doyon's door. That act embodied some kind of warning or threat, obviously, but what was it about? The Grandmother seemed genuinely mystified and claimed that Belle viewed the arrival of the pelts as weird but unimportant. My gut told me the hides must be connected with the shooting, but I couldn't be sure. Maybe their message had something to do with Belle's trap lines. A dispute over territory, perhaps? Would that kind of argument lead to attempted murder? In the Lower 48, sure, but not in Tanana. Not yet.

"I'm not really certain what I'm looking for." I crossed my arms against the laboratory chill and hiked a hip onto the stool of her microscope table. "I guess figuring out where that wolf came from is the place to start. What are the chances of that?"

Her shoulders rose in a shrug. "Slim." Then she lifted the skin of one leg and ran a thumb over the claws. "But worth a try. I'll have to destroy these claws."

"No problem. That pelt's not trophy class." I wiggled myself into a more comfortable position on the stool. "What'll you do?"

"Stable isotope tracing." Marisa's face broke into an eager smile. She hadn't changed much since our graduate school days at Berkeley. Then and now, the only things that excited her were the latest techniques and the latest technology. "This technique has taken the guesswork out of food chains. And with a source of keratin like these claws, we can map the carbon flow right down to seasonal migrations."

Meaning her answer might be a lot more specific than even my wildest dream. Now *that* was exciting! Which was why I started shivering. "How's it work?"

Marisa's eyes lit with enthusiasm. "I don't need to remind a biologist that each primary producer has a signature ratio of carbon isotopes that remains recognizable as it climbs the food chain, right?"

Even as I nodded, I shuffled mental index cards to come up with a translation. At the base of the planet's food chain are the primary producers— the green plants on land and the phytoplankton in the sea—that use sunlight to build food molecules of water and carbon dioxide.

Still, I nodded. Each primary producer contains slightly different percentages of carbon 12 and carbon 13, percentages that can be expressed as a ratio that doesn't change even after the primary producer is chewed and converted into animal tissue.

Still nodding but now with understanding. "Right."

By that time, Marisa's head bobbed in time with my own. She jerked to a stop and then waved the wolf's claws at me. "The great thing about keratin is that the nutrients are sequenced in the order of consumption."

Another wave of the wolf's claw, this time in triumph. "If you know the rate of growth of the sample tissue, you know what nutrients were consumed *and* when."

Such elegant simplicity is often the hallmark of good science. I wondered who'd figured it out, but didn't ask. I had a sudden urge to reestablish my own technical credentials. "I suppose a mass spectrometer reads the carbon dioxide?"

"Yeah." The light in Marisa Dorn's eyes died away. The technique might be new and exciting, but the technology was definitely old hat. "I'll get one of the grad students working on it tomorrow."

By the time that tomorrow dawned in Fairbanks, I'd flown down to Valdez to conduct a tutorial of my own for a half-dozen willing learners whose faces revealed the interest and intensity of committed activists. The topic of my how-to was rescuing oiled birds and animals, a subject many Alaskans reluctantly mastered in the aftermath of the Exxon Valdez disaster. Although my audience obviously cared deeply, having forked over big bucks for their ecovacations, I decided to open with the most recent numbers, just in case any of them were tempted to wonder why we fussed over a couple of murres or otters.

"Four months after the spill, having searched roughly five percent of the area affected by Exxon's oil, more than twenty-eight thousand oiled birds had been collected, including one hundred eighteen bald eagles." I spun a slow half-circle, making eye contact with all of my listeners. "Most were DOA. Only six hundred twenty-seven birds survived rescue long enough to be released."

A murmur of concern rose from the group, just as I'd hoped. American culture is so attuned to questions of how much and how many that numbers often replace dialogue.

"During that same period, eight hundred eighty-five sea otters were found, of which number twenty-six survived cleaning and were eventually released."

"That's an outrage!" A flush rouged Mildred Fenwick's withered cheeks. At sixty-five, the courtly New Jersey matron was the oldest of the group. "A survival rate of two percent for birds and barely three percent for otters! An outrage, I say!"

I gave the old lady a grim nod. "Damage estimates put the death toll as high as fifty-five hundred for sea otters and five hundred eighty thousand for birds. Add to those numbers the continuing losses through reproductive failures and what you've got is a catastrophe." Another slowly spun half-circle. "For the first time in my life, I witnessed an event that truly had catastrophic consequences."

Outrage fueled the group's intensity and steeled their determination to be ready should a similar disaster befall the rivers or sea near their homes. I gave each of them a Rubbermaid basin, a pair of elbow-length rubber gloves, and a small bottle of Dawn detergent.

"Don't settle for anything but Dawn." I measured enough to mix up a one-percent solution in warm water. "Their ad campaign is no lie. Cuts grease and still gentle. A couple of hundred birds and a handful of otters can testify that when the oil hits the water, nothing beats Dawn."

I passed out six stuffed mallards and the harsh reek of hydrocarbons invaded the air. A bright-eyed young coed from Oregon shrank back from her specimen. "Gag! It's a wonder the poor things don't suffocate."

"Some do." I set up the last piece of equipment, a Water Pik that we'd all share. "As usual, time helps. The light-end toxics evaporate, leaving the heavier stuff behind—waxes, paraffins, and asphaltenes."

I plopped the coed's duck in her basin and dipped some water over the oiled feathers with a cupped hand. "What saves us is that oil and water don't mix. Tracking down the globs of oil is the trick. You can swab the spots with a Q-tip dipped in detergent or flush it out with a little blast from the Water Pik."

Like true first-timers, all six eagerly went to work on their mallards, sudsing and swabbing and spritzing. I cruised from table to table with the Water Pik. By the time I reached the last of my students, the enormity of the task had become apparent to all.

Mildred Fenwick voiced their concern. "I find this task tedious in the extreme. In my experience, only actual nitpicking might be worse." Her shudder was most ladylike. "The one time my children had lice, I thought I'd go mad and finally shaved their heads! No such simple solution in this case, I fear."

"Nitpickers are exactly who we want for this job." I fluffed a feather and searched out a tiny globule of oil. "A neglected spot can cause hypothermia, which means death. Especially for otters."

"We have otters rescued from the spill back home at the aquarium in Newport." The Oregon coed grinned. "They're sooo cute. And really playful!"

"And lucky." I hated to replace her beautiful smile with a frown, but my job made that mandatory. "The unlucky otters foamed at the mouth, and gasped and rattled at the end. The vets who did the postmortems found their livers crumbled at the touch, and their lungs had blown, leaving the tissue looking like broccoli."

The coed blinked a couple of times fast and looked down at her duck, sudsing with a slow hand. I gave her a little pat and moved on. "The key is triage. The hopeless should be euthanized immediately."

I headed toward my briefcase on a chair across the room. "Survivors need plenty of rest and special handling."

Digging between files, I came up with the booklets of rescue guidelines devised by a committee of sympathetic vets, and gave one to each participant. "Electrolytes twice a day. And for otters, immediate sedation before pumping them full of activated charcoal to absorb the toxic hydrocarbons from the ingested oil."

When the workshop ended, Mildred Fenwick stayed behind to help me clean up. I pegged her as a birder, probably big in her local Audubon chapter, but when I asked about her next stop, her answer surprised me.

"I'll be spending the next few weeks digging in

the interior." She dipped her sponge in a fresh basin of suds before attacking a greasy tabletop with precise strokes. "I'm sure you know the area. The Nowitna refuge?"

"Not only do I know it, I'm heading there myself." When she moved to the next table, I trailed along behind with the soapy water. "What are you digging for? Agates?"

She laughed lightly with a sound as silvery as the hair on her head. "Heavens, no. It's an archaeological dig led by Dr. Preston Waite. An absolutely brilliant man. Do you know him?"

I didn't and said as much, marveling all the while over Mildred Fenwick. What a dame! While the rest of her generation packed their Winnebagos or cruised the golf courses, this compact no-nonsense "lady"—no other word for it—was up to her elbows in the sweatier side of science. Absolutely irresistible. "What are you looking for?"

"A revolution!" Her eyes gleamed with enthusiasm, and she squeezed out her sponge with a flourish. "We're searching for evidence to prove that man inhabited this hemisphere at least forty thousand years ago!"

I emptied the basin in the sink and rinsed it with fresh water. "I thought twelve thousand years was the accepted date of the land-bridge crossing."

"Not for long." Mildred Fenwick set her sponge alongside the sink and wiped her hands on paper towels. "For years, Preston Waite stood alone against the conventional wisdom, lacking both allies and artifacts in his battle for truth."

She squared her shoulders. "Now he's an old man, at the end of his career, and allies have finally appeared. It's only fair that he receive the credit. He deserves it."

I touched her arm gently. "Science is a series of tiny but key steps which lay the groundwork for a big leap. Too often the tiny steps are overlooked."

"Nobody understands that better than Preston Waite." She shook her head sadly. "Sometimes I think he'd do anything to get this settled before he dies."

8

For all of our "progress," science still broods over some pretty tantalizing mysteries, but even one dating from the Ice Age couldn't capture my attention that day. The only mystery I cared about was who shot Belle Doyon. On the plane ferrying me over the mountains from Valdez, I organized my thoughts and jotted some notes. My list of musts for my short stay in Anchorage focused on answers: "Must ask Matt Sheridan what's happening re: investigation; Must ask John Doyon his suspects re: Belle targeted for oil; Must ask medicos Belle prognosis re: talk? survive?" With only a few hours between flights, I had no time to waste and bee-lined through the terminal to the 4-Runner parked in the far corner of the long-term lot.

The rig started up with a blast of hip-hop from one of Jake's tapes. I ejected the cassette and found the radio tuned to classic Tanya Tucker. That good fortune turned into a streak of luck when I wheeled into midmorning traffic on Northern Lights Boulevard: green lights all the way to the hospital, a vacant parking slot close to the main entrance, an Up elevator with open doors in the lobby, and an eager volunteer at the ICU waiting room who gushed when I asked to see Belle.

"Why, hon, of course you can see her." The load of bangle bracelets on her arm jangled when she reached for the phone. "I'll just call back there to let them know you're coming."

I paused in the doorway to Belle's room, making a quick survey while a thin-lipped nurse with impersonal hands straightened my friend's pillow and sheet. Against that starched and perfect white, Belle's face looked like an ugly smudge, greening toward yellow as the swelling subsided. She no longer moaned in counterpoint to the machines but still required life support. From a technological standpoint, a respirator can assist breathing forever, but in practice patients do become dependent and lose their viability. Meaning they can't live without the machine.

Before I could ask the obvious question, the nurse brushed past, tossing me one cool glance and two sharp words. "Five minutes."

I hurried to the bed, hoping to find a spark of recognition in Belle's dark eyes, which stared out from between puffed and bruised lids. "Belle? It's Lauren. Can you hear me, Belle? Can you see me? Belle?"

Her gaze shifted toward me, and for a moment, I thought she knew me. But Belle was beyond seeing, beyond knowing. My hope fizzled into a lingering ache. Her gaze aimlessly wandered—to me, through me, past me—with random involuntary movement that originated in the deepest recess of her brain. Alive, but barely. And quite possibly no more than a husk of my friend, emptied now of Belle's unique consciousness.

I slid her hand into mine. Her fingers clenched and again my heart soared. Then her fingers went slack. Squeezed again and then relaxed. Squeeze, relax, squeeze, relax. Another involuntary movement. Damn.

I lifted my head, blinking back tears, staring at the flashing numbers and scrolling lines of the miracle machines, seeing without understanding the electronic blips that represented Belle's beating heart. And in my hand, her fingers squeezed and relaxed, squeezed and relaxed, squeezed and relaxed in constant rhythm, matching the electronic blips.

Matching rhythm!

In that instant, my perceptions merged and I knew. As Belle's heart beat the rhythm of life, her hand kept time. Flub, dub. Squeeze, relax. Flub, dub. Squeeze, relax. Involuntary movement? *NO!* I knew Belle was still in there. I knew that burrowed deep inside that battered and bleeding brain, my friend survived.

Ever so gently, I squeezed back. The true language of the universe may be rhythm. All matter possesses a signature vibration. Or rhythm. All life exists within cycles. Or rhythms. Day and night, summer and winter, birth and death—those are the rhythms of life.

I matched Belle squeeze for squeeze. My friend had retreated from her grave injury, drawn back from the pain, found sanctuary in a primal refuge deep within. There is no life without a beating heart, so all of Belle's energy now focused on maintaining that rhythm. Squeeze, relax, flub, dub—the backbeat of life.

I twined our hands until my wrist lay against Belle's and willed my pulse to entrain with hers. Nearly four hundred years ago, a Dutchman named Christian Huygens discovered that two clocks placed side by side will soon tick in perfect synchrony. Modern science finds nature highly efficient and speculates that entrainment occurs because pulsing together requires less energy than pulsing in opposition. If so, my pulse could help strengthen Belle's heart. And as her strength grew, the focus of her energy would expand.

"Keep squeezing, Belle." I glanced at the respirator. First the heart, then the lungs. "And add another rhythm. When you can, start breathing, Belle." After the lungs, eyes to see and ears to hear, but not too fast. "Squeeze and breathe, Belle. For now, it's enough to squeeze and to breathe."

Sometimes five minutes lasts forever. As our hands squeezed in rhythm and our wrists pulsed in time, my apprehension receded and serenity flowed through me like a cool and soothing fog. I can't really explain how it happened, but I found peace in that sterile ICU room, a new tranquility, and somehow Belle had been my guide.

"I said five minutes!" Big Nurse stormed into the room, armed with a huge and quivering syringe. "And that was almost an hour ago!"

One final squeeze, then I disengaged my hand and lowered Belle's onto her bed. Big Nurse emptied the syringe into an intravenous line, adjusted a few knobs, and then glared at me again. "You'll have to leave now."

I swept past her but paused just outside the door. Although Belle had answered my question about survival, I did have another. "Do the doctors have any idea when she'll be able to talk?"

"When?" Big Nurse snorted in my face. "*If* is more like it. Are you a member of the family?"

For once, I remained calm in the face of extreme high-handedness. Insolence couldn't stir the tranquil surface of my serenity. I didn't even have to fake the smile. "Forget it."

No way could I forget Belle's attacker. I swung by the offices of the Tanana Native Corporation to quiz John Doyon on his suspicions that Belle's injury might be related to the proposal to lease oil rights on TNC's subsistence lands. John's tired handshake, doughy skin, and weary eyes told me he didn't share my faith that his sister would survive. "Are you still sleeping at the hospital?"

He slumped into the chair behind his desk and nodded. "I don't want her to be alone. Somebody has to be there at all times."

Looked like somebody goofed, but I couldn't tell John that. Good thing I'd resisted the urge to blurt out my certainty that Belle still inhabited her body. Not that John necessarily would have believed me. He might be Athabascan, but he puts his trust in the white man's medicine. And I'll admit that the farther I got from the hospital, the more tenuous my belief seemed. Still, the essence of belief is trust, and I trusted myself. I knew Belle was still in there. That was enough for me.

I brought John up to date on the Grandmother and Jake and their doings at fish camp. He actually smiled at my description of our boat ride—proud Jake, blissful Grandmother, and terrified Lauren. He seemed relieved to hear that the fish camp buildings had lasted through another winter and that the fish wheel needed only minor repairs. That left only one subject—the real purpose of my visit—which I eased into under the pretense of more news.

"The Grandmother gave me one of the wolf pelts to drop off at the university in Fairbanks for analysis." I chose that moment to roll up the long sleeves of my blouse, trying for casual. "Have you heard anything more from the police?"

He shrugged. "Nothing important. They have no idea who did it."

I combed a hand through my hair, oh-so-relaxed and conversational. "What about those oil leases? Who's your main opposition?"

Again he shrugged. "Until we vote, it's hard to know who is opposed. Probably some on the vil-

71

lage council, although the only one I'm sure of is Eleanor Demissov."

Before I had a chance to respond, John continued in an entirely new direction.

"Those wolf pelts." He cleared his throat. "Belle did have trouble about a trapline with a fellow named Fabian Lavigne. But that was years ago. And they worked it out."

Jackpot! Take your pick—oil or furs. Either one could cause some very hard feelings. Suddenly I had two theories and two suspects and a monumental urge to get back to Tanana and onto the case. Masking the true nature of my interest expended the last of my ingenuity. To make my escape, I used the oldest trick in the book: a horrified glance at my wristwatch. Trust a twentieth-century executive to understand the notion of running to catch a plane. I was out of John Doyon's office and into my 4-Runner in record time.

The sun face on my watch really had dipped past noon, so I wouldn't have time to stop by Matt Sheridan's office at Anchorage police headquarters. Back at the airport, I detoured to a bank of telephones and dialed him up. My watch ticked off the minutes as my call made the rounds at Anchorage PD, shuttled from office to office by well-meaning souls who thought Matt Sheridan might be—with the chief? In the lab? Over at major crimes? Maybe at records? Two harried businessmen down the line each managed to complete a couple of long-distance calls before mine even connected. By the time my man had been located in the property room, I had a new question. "Why did I decide that putting a car phone in the 4-Runner was too bourgeois for words?"

Matt Sheridan's warm baritone chuckled from the receiver. "Bourgeois? Now there's a word I haven't heard for a while. Looks like you tree-hugging radicals really are red."

I kept it light. "Not necessarily. But if I were, would it make a difference?"

"Naw. We won the Cold War, remember? Even J. Edgar's shock troops are in the market for a new threat to the nation." He snickered. "My money's on an old stalwart—industrial espionage. Also known as those G-D Japs."

I turned my back to the Asian man in the next booth. "Is that why they all carry cameras?"

He barked with laughter. "You got it."

I waited for the rumble of laughter to fade before telling him what I wanted. "I wondered if you'd heard anything about that shooting up in Tanana? Victim is Belle Doyon?"

"State cops caught that one."

"I know, but I thought maybe you heard something."

He sighed. Deeply. "Are you planning to play cops and robbers again?"

"No." My turn to sigh. Deeply. "Belle's a friend. You're a friend. So I thought I'd ask."

He paused long enough to have me worried. Alaska Airlines announced an arrival and Northwest Orient gave a final boarding call before he finally answered. "I've heard the bullets were definitely .25s, and there are no suspects."

".25s? What does that mean?"

"That's caliber, Lauren. As in .25 caliber. Which is a little unusual."

"Unusual?" I bit, just as he wanted. Even the best of men love to show off about guns and can't resist the urge to educate a woman. "What does *that* mean?"

"Not too many models available. And .25's never been a popular caliber. You just don't see that many."

My "hhhmmm" turned out to be too noncommittal for my friend the detective. He started asking questions of his own. "What's that mean, Lauren? What are you planning?"

I tried for a combination of innocence and naïveté. "I'm not planning anything. I just wanted to know."

Although he persisted for a few more minutes, I refused to be lured into a revelation. But Matt Sheridan knew. He ended our call with a little unasked-for advice. "Carry the Colt this time, Lauren. And if you have to, use it."

9

A haze of fine dust clouded the air in front of Eleanor Demissov's cabin, stirred up not by the ubiquitous dogs of the village but by a little boy scrabbling in the dirt. I slowed my approach, studying the dark head that bent over a collection of dented trucks and admiring the sound effects of rumbling engines and screeching tires. Not bad for a kid whose exposure to mechanized land transport probably began with snow machines and ended with three-wheelers. The child's presence offered reassurance. Eleanor Demissov might be a witch, but she was also a mother. Perhaps in motherhood we could find common ground.

I stopped a couple of feet from the little boy, shifting the stiff wolf pelt to my left hand and leaving my right hand free to shake. The smaller the child, the more they appreciate an adult approach. "Hello, young man."

He reacted in slow motion, mouth motoring and hands propelling for several seconds after I spoke. First, turn off the motors. Then stop the trucks. And then look up at the stranger with the fading smile.

Observation: small, round wide-set eyes; thin, ungrooved upper lip; little head; flat face.

Hypothesis: fetal alcohol syndrome.

Verification would have to wait because the wolf pelt in my hand had caught the boy's interest. He pointed a stubby finger. "Whas dat?"

"Fur." I held the pelt out to him. "From a wolf."

He inched forward on his knees and prodded the stiff pelt. "Bad fur. Hard."

I nodded theatrically and lifted my shoulders into an outsize shrug. "That's true. I'm sure your mother's furs are much nicer. Very good."

He scrunched up his eyes, wrinkling his forehead. "Mother?"

As if in answer, Eleanor Demissov appeared in the doorway. Her dark eyes swept over me before focusing on the boy at my feet. "Adam. Get your basket."

After giving the wolf pelt one last touch, Adam climbed to his feet and moved past her into the cabin. Eleanor Demissov remained in the doorway, silent and still.

However unwelcome, I decided not to act the part of the intruder. Genuine interest and a shy smile sounded right. "Your son?"

Old Stone-face took her time about answering. Probably weighing pros and cons, although the smidgen of information she finally provided seemed harmless enough. "My sister's son."

"Aahh, a nephew." My nod might have been a tad too vigorous. And the next question definitely qualified as nosy. "Where's she?"

Her eyes flashed fire. "Drunk." She spat the word. And then two more. "Or dead."

I braved those angry flames, leveling my eyes on hers. "I'm so sorry."

Adam reappeared beside her before she had a chance to heap scorn upon me. He jumped to the ground and hoisted a willow basket in my direction. "For berry."

He spun back to Eleanor, wobbling like a spent top as he flung a finger in my direction. "Her come, too."

She opened her mouth to object, but I snatched the little hand, tugging him toward me. "That's a great idea, Adam. I love picking berries!"

So I spent the long, golden afternoon berrying with a little boy who couldn't say much and an angry woman who wouldn't say anything. And having a marvelous time. Once I got over my initial grizzly bear gooseflesh, that is. Berry patches make prime grizzly habitat since all *Ursidae* crave the northern summer's sweetest treat. Even the great *Ursus maritimus* scarfs any berries that can be found in his polar home.

I followed Adam from bush to bush, helping fill his basket along with my pail. One handful for

Adam, one handful for Lauren, one moment to check for bears by carefully surveying the shadowed edges of the boggy clearing. The incessant hum of insects only heightened my jitters. Who could hear a bear amid all the damned buzzing? But for once I truly appreciated mosquitoes because their bites kept me alert. I'd already lost one friend to a grizzly and didn't plan to lose another. I took some comfort in knowing Adam's slowness kept him within snatching range. I also felt some confidence in knowing the Colt on my hip could stop a grizzly with one shot.

My anxiety must have shown because I caught Eleanor Demissov smirking as she watched me out of the corner of her eye. Maybe her sense of superiority chiseled the first crack in the wall between us. Maybe my bona fide enjoyment of her nephew's company knocked off a couple of bricks. Or maybe she just got used to me. However it happened, by the time we'd filled a recycled pickle barrel with blueberries, Eleanor was ready—if not to be friends—at least to stop being enemies.

I carried a final pail of fruit to the stout plastic barrel and dumped the berries. Adam followed, plopping onto the ground beside the cache to snack from his basket. He picked over the berries, eating them one by one. Eleanor studied him for a moment before dumping her own final pail.

I nodded at the barrel. "That's a lot of blueberry pancakes."

She surprised me by flashing a brilliant smile. "I like my berries in fat."

I returned her smile, although the thought of eating blueberries floating in oil almost gagged me. Non-natives call the concoction Eskimo ice cream, a terminology that now violates the reigning PC. "How do we get this home? I think it's too heavy, even for two of us."

She settled the lid on top and screwed it down tight. "After the snow, I'll come for the berries."

"Won't the bears get into the barrel?"

Eleanor flung her arms wide to embrace the many bushes thickly studded with berries. "Not with such plenty. By the time Raven strips the last bush, Bear will be asleep in his den."

She pulled Adam to his feet and herded him toward the spot where the trail through the spruce forest entered the clearing. I detoured far enough to retrieve the pelt I'd left at the foot of a young white birch and then trotted to catch up. Eleanor tossed a glance over her shoulder. "Why do you bring that pelt?"

"To ask you about it." I edged into position beside her, trying to match my steps to hers. "The Grandmother found this pelt and another on her doorstep before the attack on Belle. I thought maybe this was hers."

That threw a hitch into her gait. Adam didn't seem to notice and darted ahead to swing a stick against a stout spruce trunk. His aunt frowned. "Belle doesn't trap *teekkona.*"

Which threw a hitch into my gait. And I frowned. "Why do you say that?"

"Hutlaanee!" She snorted disgust at the depth of

79

my ignorance. "From distant time, woman must not hunt wolf or trap wolf or skin wolf. It is taboo."

Up ahead, Adam veered off the path to investigate a scurry in the underbrush. Eleanor stopped at the place where he'd left the path and waited without complaint. Maybe impatience is the hallmark only of cultures that live by the clock.

The pause allowed me to gather my thoughts. One thing I knew for sure about Belle Doyon: no way she'd break a taboo. She followed the old ways from the heart and to the last detail. So the only question I had was why wolf was taboo for women.

Eleanor didn't hesitate to explain. "In distant times, wolf was human. Once a wolf with two wolf wives took a human girl, too. After a boy was born to the girl, the wolf killed his first wives. But their spirits remained to kill the girl wife and eat her insides. Since then, woman must not touch wolf until she is too old for children."

Adam barreled out of the woods and back onto the path, prompting a smile from his aunt as we fell into step behind him. Like many preindustrial cultures, the *Dene* cherish procreation because they have always existed on the brink of extinction. Survival of the race is no joke to subsistence peoples.

I ran a hand over the brittle fur of the pelt as we followed the trail around an old growth spruce. No man or woman had touched this wolf since skinning it. The pelt had been left dry and dead, showing none of the supple vitality that came with expert working and curing. "Eleanor, who do you suppose skinned the wolf?"

"Not one of us, I think." She raised one hand and then the other. *"Teekkona* is powerful. To waste even one life brings much danger, but two? Fur is also very valuable. Two pelts is twice the loss."

Up ahead, Adam whooped into a gallop, spilling blueberries across the widening trail. Eleanor and I walked the last few yards in silence, joining him at the head of the typical bush road: two rutted tracks divided by a rock-studded hump of earth that bore the fresh scrapes and gouges of recent passage.

Eleanor grabbed Adam's hand and stepped up the pace. Around the next bend, we overtook a rusting Ford pickup carrying two men, a native behind the wheel and a white man behind a USGS topo map.

Dropping Adam's hand, she darted forward with an angry growl. I put a hand on the boy's thin shoulder, drawing him close as his aunt snagged a rock from the dusty road and pitched it at the pickup. Adam flinched into me when the rock came down hard, sending up a chime as it skittered across the pickup bed and clanged off the sides. As the truck drew to a stop, I tightened my grip on the boy while Eleanor strutted forward to confront the two men who piled out of the cab.

The white man swiped the baseball cap off his head, gave her a lazy grin, and drawled pure Texan. "Now, Miss Demissov, you have no call to throw rocks at us. This here's a public way."

Eleanor positively bristled. "And you have no call to survey this land. Each acre belongs to the village corporation, and the mineral rights are not for sale."

I came up beside her, holding Adam close, although the boy seemed more curious than frightened. The Texan threw me a nod and gave me a ma'am before following up with Eleanor. "Not yet maybe, but no harm done. A little look-see never hurt nobody."

She held her ground and her tongue, eyeing the native driver, who coughed and fidgeted by the cab. The Texan gave me a once-over as he settled the ball cap over his thick gray hair. He ma'amed us again and then climbed back into the truck, signaling the driver to move on.

Adam slipped out from under my arm and skipped away, scuffing up dust as he twirled down the road. Eleanor glared after the pickup until the Ford disappeared around the next bend. Then she turned her dark, troubled eyes on me and spat out one word. "Oil."

I took a deep breath and let it out slowly. "I think we're on the same side. Oil development can only harm your subsistence lands."

She spread her arms to embrace the huge sweep of forest rising away from us in tiered ridges. "We asked for our land and they gave us corporations. One hundred shares for everyone. Now our people are dying and our heritage is traded away, share by share."

"John Doyon says you call it genocide."

"Our people and families are splintered and confused. The young go your way and the elders fall silent." She shrugged and then allowed her shoulders to slump. "Your people came first for furs, then for gold, and now for oil."

She turned back to me, eyes bleak. "They didn't stop then and they won't stop now. Your people won't stop until they get it all."

10

Trust a Texan to settle on my gun as a conversational gambit. As I waited for a trickle of hot water to fill the tub for my load of whites, the oil man with the gray hair and false courtesy ambled into the village laundry toting a worn canvas duffel. Although he'd ma'amed me a few hours earlier, I looked right through him. Not that my incivility deterred him in the slightest. He strolled the short aisle between the washers and dryers, lowered the duffel to the cracked cement floor, and nodded at the holster riding my right thigh. "You carry that just for show? Or for real?"

For a second, I struggled with the impulse to give him a Hollywood answer à la the Calamity Jane and Annie Oakley movies of my youth, to whip out that .45 and—*with one blast*—dot the *i* on the Pepsi sign hanging over the bank of dryers. Life should be so sweet! As a slew of feminist scholars have pointed out, the purpose of that stock scene wasn't to illustrate the good old gal's marksmanship. The purpose was to socialize the audience of "nice" impressionable girls by demonstrating the consequences of the heroine's lack of manners and decorum: No manners equals no man. To this day, I am constitutionally unable to say something rude on purpose. (Except, of course, to my nearest and dearest, but that's another story.) In the end, I played it straight. "For real. I spend a lot of time in the bush."

Just then, the washing machine switched from gurgling to churning, vibrating with the effort. I dumped in the last of my vending machine detergent and waited for "the patented surgilator action" to suds up before lowering the lid. At the same time, I braced for the blow.

Instead of the disparagement I expected, the Texan offered praise. "Good choice. You need that stopping power."

Surprise struck me dumb. All I could do was watch as he positioned himself between two washing machines, pulled open his duffel, and sorted his laundry into the washers as light and dark loads. Not once did he ask for my advice. Not in sorting. Not in temperature selection. Not even in choosing a detergent! And when he didn't pull the knob under my brand, his choice struck me as a silent rebuke. Oh, the power of gender role stereotypes. Ridiculous!

When the Texan finished with his washing machines, he turned back to me, offering his hand. After wc'd exchanged handshakes and names, George Baker leaned back against his washer, folded his arms, and picked up the earlier thread of our conversation.

"Always a pleasure to find commonsense white folks in the bush, especially a woman." He chewed on his lower lip and shook his head slowly. "Not three weeks ago we damn near lost two ladies to a griz. Fine-looking pair, but dumber than dirt."

Baker managed to raise my hackles along with my interest. Still, I couldn't resist asking for more. My fascination with grizzly bears goes way beyond morbid curiosity.

"Spotted them from a chopper when we were doing a survey east of here a ways, over around the Yukon Flats. Against all that green, those ladies stood out like two gumdrops laying on the lawn." He grinned and the bronze skin around his eyes creased into a fine web of wrinkles. "Pink hat, yellow anorak, lavender backpack—I never saw such gear before. And all of it just bought, of course."

Definitely upscale, probably from Outside and, in all likelihood, feminist and/or separatist. Part of a new breed of interior trekkers who come into the country on a personal or spiritual quest, only to learn that nature can be downright nasty. Every year, a couple return home in baggage. And every year, Alaskans marvel that so very few of the *cheechako* actually come to grief.

"On our first pass, we noticed the griz about a quarter mile behind them but thought nothing of it. There's bears all through that country." He cocked an eyebrow at me. "Second time over, he's still coming. And closing the gap."

I couldn't suppress a shiver, and Baker couldn't help but notice. Close calls do that to you. After my near miss a few weeks earlier, my attitude toward grizzlies could never be sanguine. I threw him a weak smile. "Bears give me the willies."

He smiled back. "Me too. But not those ladies. We buzzed them, figuring to drive off the griz. And what do they do?" He spread his arms wide, all outraged innocence. "Throw rocks at us, like your friend, Eleanor Demissov. And curse us out. And then, they charge back down that trail, heading straight for that griz!" He heaved a deep sigh and refolded his arms. "So the flyboy takes the chopper down to the treetops while I load the Remington."

True to my ideals, I couldn't help ruining George Baker's story by blurting the obvious question. "You didn't kill the bear?"

He slapped a hand over his heart and opened his eyes wide. There's a bit of the ham in all true sons of Texas. "It really is true. You preservationists do care more for animals than for people."

"Cut the crap, George." I softened my words with a slight smile. "Did you kill that bear?"

He snorted. "Not likely. That old griz heard those women coming long before the ladies arrived. He skedaddled. But they spotted his prints and fresh scat. Next thing you know, they're waving like mad and shouting pretty pleases like a couple of Fourth Avenue whores."

He tossed back his head, laughing with such delight that even I felt tickled. Trust a Texan to confound your cherished stereotypes, humanize what you would demonize, and charm you within an inch of abandoning your convictions. I had to force myself to remember that George Baker was an enemy, an outrider for the worst of all land rapers—Big Oil.

I'd almost succeeded in armoring myself against him when a muddy three-wheeler roared up to the laundry. An unkempt Athabascan man staggered off the machine and lurched into the doorway. Bracing hands on the jambs, he closed his eyes and stood there swaying. After a few moments, he opened his eyes, glanced around the small laundry, mumbled something unintelligible, staggered back to his machine, and roared off.

"Jesus." A trace of despair roughened George Baker's drawl. "No wonder they hate us. No wonder they fear us."

"Spare me the crocodile tears, cowboy." I stomped a foot in genuine outrage. "Unless you're ready to tear up your topo maps and torch your survey findings, why don't you just give it a rest?"

Put it down to either a long fuse or the temperament of a saint. Instead of sticking out his chin and getting belligerent, George Baker reasoned with me. He took hold of my hand, looked me straight in the eye, and tried to make me understand. "Way

I figure it, as long as there's oil to be had, sooner or later somebody's going to pump it. And, in this case, sooner is better than later."

Resisting the urge to drop my gaze or yank my hand away, I stood fast, remembering my mother's dictum that no one learns anything when they're talking.

"See, the native's big fight won't be with guys like me. Their big fight's with people like you, who want to turn Alaska into a game park, and with the white natives who want a share in subsistence."

His argument wasn't new. I'd been over the same territory with John Doyon many times. Tree huggers adore the artsy-fartsy side of subsistence, the baskets and beadwork and soapstone carving, but they despise the fishing, hunting, and trapping that lie at the very heart of the lifestyle. And many who worship the wild have dedicated their efforts to ending the slaughter.

"You know, we brought these people a lot of stuff they don't really need. Cable television. Potato chips. Rock and roll. A whole bunch of dumb stuff that took them away from the land. And without the land, these people are dead. Or drunk."

His words echoed those of Eleanor Demissov, and I told him so. "I'll have to tell her you're not such a bad guy after all. Maybe she'll stop throwing rocks."

He shook his head and gave me a sad little smile. "Anger like hers is good. Righteous anger gives strength. Bitter anger's the one to watch out for. That can get scary."

"You scared? I don't believe it." I pulled my hand free and anchored it on my hip. "When's the last time that happened?"

"Last time I ran into a white trapper. About a week ago, in fact." He gestured again at my gun. "Which is another reason I always carry one of those in the bush. I had the feeling he would have dropped me in second if he thought he could get away with it."

A frisson of unease lifted the hair on my neck. Exactly the thought of Belle's attacker. Who had actually gotten away with it. So far, at least. "You can't be serious. I mean, did he even know you?"

"Only by reputation. He knew I worked in oil and that was enough." He shrugged. "Fabian Lavigne hates the oil industry."

Fabian Lavigne! John Doyon had mentioned the same trapper. And the fact that Belle once had a run-in with him. I decided to press the point. "Plenty of folks hate the oil industry, but not enough to start killing people."

"True." Again he shrugged. "But Fabian Lavigne's a hater. He hates oil. He hates natives. And he hates environmentalists. Far as I can tell, he hates just about everybody. And that's kind of scary."

11

Fabian Lavigne looked like he'd stepped out of the pages of one of Jack London's Klondike stories. A scruffy blond beard cascaded over his barrel chest and one cheek bulged with a plug of tobacco. Every couple of minutes he pursed his lips and fired a burst of spit before bending back over the machine parts strewn across the table of his outdoor workshop. The forearms knotted with muscles suggested brute strength, but his heavily calloused fingers moved over the disassembled engine with a delicate precision. Today's career mountain men are fluent in small-engine repair, carpentry, guns, and survival gear, all of which leaves little time for the niceties of polite society.

He saw me coming as soon as I passed the last cabin in the village but took no action until I stepped onto his property. When my foot touched his ground, Fabian Lavigne lifted his shaggy head and stared across a dusty "yard" littered with dented oil drums, used lumber, and scrap metal. "No soliciting."

I ignored his bark and instead studied his cabin. The classic trapper exterior featured plywood sheathing over a log frame and a pair of mismatched double-hung windows. Inside there'd be a rusty old stove, a bed built into one wall, a jumble of gear festooned from the rafters, and at least a yard of well-thumbed and well-loved books.

"Are you deaf or are you nuts?" Lavigne rose from his stool, squaring shoulders that proved to be very broad, and lifting that shaggy head to an impressive height. "I said 'no soliciting,' and I mean it."

"I'm sure you do." I plastered a brilliant smile on my face as I picked my way through the clutter surrounding his worktable. I tucked the wolf pelt under an arm and stuck out my hand. "My name's Lauren Maxwell, and I'm not soliciting."

Most men wouldn't have taken my hand until they'd wiped the grease off their own, but not Fabian Lavigne. His mean streak showed in the pleasure he took in that soiled and bone-crushing handshake. I did my best not to wince at his wringing or his words. "Even so, that don't mean you're welcome here."

My smile faded some but didn't disappear. When his grip loosened, I jerked my hand away. "The sooner you quit bullying, the sooner I'm out of here."

His eyes narrowed and his jaw worked that chaw at a furious pace. I prepared for a roadhouse right, but instead Fabian Lavigne threw me a grin and bellowed at the cabin. "Hey, Lucille. Get some brew out here. Pronto."

A young woman with bony arms and shy eyes stepped out of the cabin, hoisting her long cotton skirt with one hand and an unlabeled quart bottle in the other. The sight of me seemed to unnerve her. She darted back into the cabin, and when she returned, two battered tin cups also hung from the hand clenching the bottle. The woman didn't greet me, meet my eyes, or exchange a word with the trapper. She just set the bottle and cups on the worktable and then disappeared back into the cabin.

Fabian Lavigne unscrewed the cap. "Lucille don't have much to say." He filled both cups with an amber liquid and pushed one in my direction. "Works a hide good, though, and cooks up a fine brew."

That much, at least, we could agree on. Even served warm, Lucille's brew tasted like bottled summer, heavy with mellow riches and lazy pleasures. I took another deep gulp and then allowed a sigh to escape. "A very fine brew indeed."

Offering a drink proved to be the limit of Fabian Lavigne's hospitality. After quaffing the last of his own, he got back to business. "What do you want here?"

No use trying to dodge a direct question from a man as suspicious as the trapper. Evasion would leave him only two choices: going ballistic or falling silent. Neither possibility appealed to me right then. "I want you to tell me what you can about this wolf pelt." I lifted the skin toward him. "The Grandmother found it on her doorstep a few days before Belle was shot."

He ignored the fur, staring across at me with steely gray eyes. "You got some nerve coming here for that."

Despite the ache in my arms, I held the pelt steady. "John Doyon told me there'd been bad feelings between you and Belle. He also said you'd settled all that a long time ago."

"John Doyon told you, did he?" Lavigne's eyes frosted over. "Did he tell you what it's like to be a white trapper in Indian country?" He punctuated the question with one staccato spit. "Did he tell you what it's like to pay a native top dollar for his cabin and then find yourself locked out of the best country because it belongs to the tribe?"

Lavigne folded his arms and chewed his plug furiously, waiting for my next move. I laid the wolf pelt aside and took my time, setting my mind on replay and carefully considering his words until I discovered my opening. Then I leaned forward, not far enough to intrude on his space but close enough to invite confession. "Sounds like your quarrel's with Belle Doyon's brother."

"With her muck-a-muck brother and that damned corporation he runs." Another hissing stream of tobacco juice. "You got that much right."

I composed my face into solemn lines, ready to

gamble. "I'm not here about him. Or about TNC. I'm here about Belle. She needs your help."

For the longest time, Fabian Lavigne just looked at me. Without chewing. Without spitting. Without talking. I stayed quiet, too. Knowing when to quit is sometimes half the battle. After a few minutes, he started chewing again. Then he spit once or twice. And finally he spoke. "When I come into this country, I thought I knew something about trapping. Did enough of it back home in Vermont. And raised there, I thought I knew something about winter, too."

He reached for my cup and filled it to brimming with Lucille's brew. "That first season I about froze. About starved, too. Seemed like I couldn't trap nothing but muskrats. And my grubstake was down to just cornmeal by the time spring come along. I was heartsick, bone weary, and mad at the world. I mean angry."

Lavigne filled his own cup with brew but didn't drink. "I aimed most of that anger at Belle Doyon. She was the best trapper in the village, of course. Seemed like she had a sixth sense. About weather, too. She brought in the richest pelts and always made it home before thirty below."

He lifted his cup, one cheek bulging with tobacco as he strained the beer through the other. "Next season I went through the ice on Bear Creek, along with my snow machine. Temperature of fifteen below and falling."

For the first time since he started talking, Fabian Lavigne looked me straight in the eye. "She found me. And she saved my life." A burst of jawing, followed by one spit. "Turned out she heard me leaving the village and followed. Told me she knew something wasn't right." More jawing and spitting. "Like I said. Belle Doyon's got a sixth sense about things."

"She sure does." I allowed myself a smile. "She taught me most of what I know about the bush. And every lesson reminds me how much I've got left to learn."

He grinned, splitting that blond beard and lifting the storm clouds from his eyes. "She taught me about trapping and weather—surviving Alaska. And I taught her about business—surviving Outside."

That surprised me. "But Belle's never been Outside."

"True enough." Lavigne's grin widened. "But that's her market. A lot bigger market than she ever figured. I taught her how to sell a pelt to a museum. I showed her where to peddle the castor glands off beavers. And I told her how much a collector's willing to pay for a skull."

I took that as my cue and again lifted the wolf pelt toward Fabian Lavigne. "What can you teach me about this wolf?"

He took the fur from me and swiveled away from the workbench until he could lay the pelt across his lap. His examination lasted about fifteen minutes and proceeded methodically, starting at the snout and ending at the tail. He stroked the fur and poked the skin. He blew gently, parting the fur of the head, the leg, the back. He rubbed the skin between thumb and index finger and stretched the pelt full-length for measurement. And just when I decided the whole performance was probably empty theatrics, he pronounced his judgment with the simplicity and solemnity of an Old Testament prophet. "Not one of Belle's."

Sixth sense or no, this scientist wanted more. "How can you tell?"

He lifted his shoulders into a shrug. "Her wolf line runs up a couple of creeks in the Tozitna drainage. Pickings have been kind of slim over there the last few seasons." He ruffled the fur with one hand. "This little doggy been eating too fine for Tozitna country."

I cocked an eyebrow at him. "If you can tell that just by looking, you must have a sixth sense, too."

"Could be." He loosed a stream of tobacco juice. "Of course, their *hutlaanee* helps some."

Hutlaanee! That word again! "What does an Athabascan taboo have to do with this pelt?"

"Belle Doyon follows the old ways. All the time we've been friendly, I've never known her to skin a wolf." He swung back to the worktable and laid the pelt on top of the machine parts. "Brung them all to me for skinning."

He flourished a final spit to underscore his point. "For certain, I never skinned this wolf."

12

The biggest problem with developing a hypothesis comes when the facts prove the theory wrong. Not that facts had anything to do with my personal acquittal of Eleanor Demissov and Fabian Lavigne. How did I know that neither the Athabascan radical nor the sourdough trapper had shot my friend Belle Doyon? Instinct told me, not evidence. My gut told me, not my head. Even as a scientist, I'm a great believer in such leaps of faith. So were big-time theorists like Galileo Galilei, Isaac Newton, and Marie Curie. I *knew* neither Eleanor nor Fabian pulled the trigger. I just couldn't prove it.

Not that I didn't try. Most of my last afternoon in Tanana was spent tracking down the local cop charged with uncovering Belle's attacker. Proving guilt or innocence fit his job description, not mine. I just wanted to offer him the benefit of my analysis and to see if he had any new information that might point me in a fresh direction. Besides, I had a few hours to kill. Four o'clock was the prearranged time for my telephone consultation with Marisa Dorn about the wolf pelt I'd left at her Fairbanks lab. And the skipper of the downriver barge that would ferry me to the Grandmother's fish camp had made it quite clear that I wasn't welcome aboard his vessel any earlier than 6 P.M. That left me more than enough time to locate Officer Simeon Frank and find out the latest. Or so I thought.

I dawdled on the way to the village offices, kicking a battered spruce cone through the road dust as I rehearsed my spiel for the lawman. I had three reasons for believing Fabian Lavigne innocent of the attack on Belle: the weapon, the wolf, and the world. Trappers working country populated by grizzly bears, moose, wolves, and other large critters want a weapon with stopping power. The .25-caliber handgun used on Belle worked fine at close range against a fragile human skull, but the same weapon aimed at a griz or a moose would be about as effective as a popgun. Trappers like Fabian Lavigne specialized in utility in all things, especially guns. No .25-caliber gun had a place in his arsenal.

A pair of all-terrain vehicles wheeled out of a side street, throwing up a thick cloud of dust that forced me to a stop. One driver slowed her three-wheeler, a blonde with reflecting sunglasses and a pristine pair of Hi-Tec hiking boots. Her partner steered his machine into a tight 360, spraying dust and pebbles from the oversized mud-season tires. The fine dust hung in the afternoon air, slowly drifting across the intersection toward the open window of a worn and sagging cabin.

The blonde saw my look and immediately caught on. "Hey, Harv, cut it out. You're making a mess."

"Whaddya mean?" Harv repositioned his pastel baseball cap and barked with laughter. "The place is a dump."

I turned a corner and walked on, suddenly eager for the first dusting of snow that always signaled the last wave of tourists. After my breathing evened out I returned to my rehearsal, moving on to my second reason: the wolf. Fabian Lavigne hadn't needed fifteen minutes to conclude that the pelt wasn't one of Belle's. He knew his own handiwork at a glance and could judge the value of a fur almost as quickly. But the trapper had taken his time over that pelt, carefully examining the fur with the lingering hand of an aficionado and the reverent eye of a true believer. Both of the pelts left at the Grandmother's door carried high-quality fur. Few trappers would waste one good fur on symbolism. And no trapper would waste two.

My detour took me down an unfamiliar street into a newer section of town. A rank of barged-in double-wides rested on concrete piers, their manufactured symmetry looking artificial and alien alongside the older log homes. In a few villages, the natives had abandoned their new homes, complaining of ailments that some ecotypes attributed to their sudden exposure to plastics and glues, the processed elements of a man-made world. The only traditional village residents to adapt universally to manufactured homes hung out under the floors and between the piers. In summer the dogs lazed in the deep shade, and in winter they burrowed out storm shelters. But just then, their wagging tails thumped a friendly beat as I wandered back toward familiar ground.

At the next corner, I paused to orient myself, checking the streets against my mental map before setting off again toward the village offices. Third and final reason Fabian Lavigne didn't shoot Belle: their world. The clash of cultures had wrought dramatic changes in the bush. Satellites provided telephones and TV. Assembly lines produced motorboats and snow machines. Junk food and welfare checks, liquor stores and indoor plumbing, medevacs and beauty pageants—all were now part of the village scene. But some things never change. Like a man slipping through a crack in the ice at fifteen below. That man expects death. When he finds salvation instead, he doesn't forget. Not ever. Fabian Lavigne hadn't forgotten and never would. Every world makes some rules inviolate. In the world Fabian Lavigne and Belle Doyon shared, no man harms his savior.

In the fashion of the new bush, the village offices boasted the freshest paint in Tanana. Back in the early seventies, Alaska's natives struck a deal with the feds that allowed construction of an oil pipeline across the state in exchange for title to forty million acres and one billion dollars. The settlement launched a municipal construction boom that lasted through the mideighties oil bust. These days, only a few villages still had enough spare cash to paint the town hall and plant pink petunias beside the door. Even fewer employed receptionists at stations just inside the foyer. Tanana's girl tossed her sleek braid over her shoulder and smiled a greeting. "Looking for anyone in particular?"

I marched up to her desk. "Officer Simeon Frank."

She stiffened, her dark eyes widening before darting glances from my face to the office doors on either side of the hall. "Is there some trouble?"

"Not at all." I tried for a reassuring smile. "I just need to talk to him. Nothing important."

"Oh, good." She relaxed into her chair. "But sort of not-so-good, too. I mean, he's not here." She shrugged. "He took the day off."

I bit back a "damn" and propped a fist on one hip. "Any chance I might catch him at home?"

The girl shook her head. "Don't think so. He planned to get some fish in today." She threw a glance over her shoulder at the clock high on the back wall. "Simeon won't get off the river for hours yet."

Which spared him from hearing my one-word defense of Eleanor Demissov's innocence. I gave the receptionist sincere thanks—How often do you get such straight answers at town hall?—and headed back outside. To me, one word said everything about Eleanor Demissov: courage. That quality was notably lacking in Belle's attacker. Siddling up to a doorstep to leave a symbolic message was an act of cowardice. A cross etched in fire, a swastika splashed in paint, a wolf stiff with blood—all were the handiwork of cowards. But Eleanor Demissov was no coward. She had the courage of her convictions, wearing her likes and dislikes on her sleeve. She reminded me of natives of my own kind: in-your-face New Yorkers. Rude but honest. And Eleanor had the courage to change, to see beyond the color of my skin and give me a second chance. Her fight was with John Doyon, not Belle, and she never pretended otherwise. Would a woman like that sneak up to the Grandmother's cabin and gun down the sister to send a message to the brother? No way! No ifs, no ands, no buts, no way.

The one place in any town certain to draw a crowd is the post office, and Tanana's mail room proved no exception to the rule. A short line of tourists snaked away from the counter, forcing villagers to dart around one end to reach the bank of locked boxes against the wall. A hearty young woman in federal green shorts toted a canvas bag up to the largest box and quickly filled it with an array of envelopes, magazines, and rolled newspapers. The U.S. Fish and Wildlife Service badge on her sleeve marked her as an overseer of the Nowitna Refuge downriver. The young man at her side was tougher to peg. Good haircut, worn but expensive boots, ninety-bazillion function watch—

a professional what? When the Nowitna woman called him Doctor, I remembered the little old lady from my oil-spill rescue seminar in Valdez. Mildred Fenwick had mentioned an archaeological dig at the Nowitna. That pegged the fellow as a scientist.

I hung back in the corner near the wall phone and considered a whole new crowd of suspects in Belle's shooting. A villager or someone from the wildlife refuge? A tourist or a member of an archaeological expedition? A villager seemed too obvious. Surely Officer Simeon Frank would have nailed a townie by now. Murders don't go unsolved very long in a village with only 415 inhabitants. But the other possibilities seemed equally ludicrous. With rape and robbery definitely not part of the picture, what motive would a tourist have for harming Belle? Or a bird person from the refuge or a bone person from the dig, either?

The clock spared me from the frustration of that puzzle by striking the hour. I dialed Marisa Dorn's number at the university in Fairbanks and waited through the usual sequence of clicks, hums, and electronic bleeps until the call went through. She answered on the first ring. "Dorn here."

"Lauren Maxwell calling from Tanana." I turned my back to the lobby. "Any luck tracing stable isotopes from the claw of my wolf?"

Her chuckle spilled into my ear, rich with triumph. "Yup. Maybe a little too much. In life, that creature was a true omnivore."

That hollowed my stomach. A slew of possibilities when all I really wanted was one. My next word came out in a groan. "Wonderful."

"Absolutely. Wonderful is the word." This time the chuckle grated. "My grad students did a wonderful job narrowing the field for me. And I did a wonderful job making the final choice."

"Choice?" I tightened my grip on the telephone. "Choice of what?"

"Primary food source." She'd stopped chuckling and started lecturing. "You wanted to know where that wolf had been. Only way to do that was to get the data on his diet. And then to isolate the primary food source. Primary food source indicates primary habitat. Lauren, you know all of this."

I sighed into the phone. "You're right. But I'm tired and not thinking too well. Just give me the upshot, will you?"

"Clethrionomys rutilus. That wolf's primary food source was the red-backed vole."

I mentally shuffled through the order of mammals, trying to locate that little mousie by range, habitat, and diet. Fortunately, Marisa Dorn had done my homework for me.

"Red-backs like the woods—deep, dark, and moist. Think mossy logs and damp berry patches and thick shrubbery."

Think? Who needed to think? That description fit only one kind of habitat: old growth forest. And in the country around Tanana, only one locale contained much old growth anymore—the Nowitna Wildlife Refuge.

Marisa had more to tell me but I'd stopped listening. As casually as you please, I swung around to face the post office lobby, eager to search out the hearty young woman from the wildlife service and the bone doctor with the good haircut.

Search? What search? He was right beside me! Literally at my elbow! Our glances locked. My heart tripped into a faster beat. What had he heard? What did he know?

He lifted a hand toward me. My breath caught in my throat. I backed away, backed myself right into the corner. He stared at me for a moment, a strange, smirking grin on his face, and let his hand drop.

I squeezed my eyes shut, turned into the corner and tried to concentrate on Marisa's voice. No such luck. I fought down my panic. The bone doctor had surprised me. That's all. There was no reason for alarm. No big deal.

And so I talked myself into opening my eyes. Then I found the courage to turn around. But the bone doctor was gone.

13

Sometimes just one look tells a Mom everything she needs to know about her kid. When the skipper of the downriver barge hailed the Grandmother's fish camp with three quick toots, my son came running. Jake bounded down the steep riverbank in four huge leaps and vaulted into the skiff. One hard pull started the outboard motor. After shoving off and steering the boat into the current, he finally raised his head. A grin as wide as the Yukon blazed across his sun-darkened face. I didn't have to see the matching sparkle in his eyes to know that my son had found his own kind of heaven.

The barge captain motioned his deckhand forward as Jake swung the skiff around the spinning fish wheel and maneuvered in close. "Fine-looking young man."

The words spoke a truth I could no longer deny.

107

In this, his thirteenth summer, my son was losing the last of his boyishness. Already, he topped my five foot seven by half an inch and chimed into a deeper register when he spoke. New flesh filled his stringy arms and legs, rounding them into muscles that bulged with the promise of mansize strength. And beneath his simple pleasure in mastering his little boat lay a maturing confidence that he could face and master the tasks of a complex world. A small cloud of regret shadowed my blooming pleasure. The man who made Jake had damn well deserved to know this young man. Poor Max. Poor Jake. Poor everyone in this sad old world.

Jake brought his boat alongside the barge, tossing a line to the deckhand and slinging another around a large cleat. After securing his boat he sprang onto the barge and trotted over to me. "Where's your stuff?"

I didn't embarrass him by insisting on a kiss, a hug, or even a greeting. I simply pointed to the backpack resting against the bulkhead, thanked the barge's skipper for the lift, and allowed the mate to offer a steadying hand as I lowered myself into the front seat of the Grandmother's skiff. Jake settled my gear into the middle of the boat before casting off. He let our boat drift for a few minutes, allowing the Yukon's current to move us away from the barge, before throttling us toward shore.

Sarah Doyon appeared at the edge of the high bench above the river, outfitted with a canvas apron stained with fish blood and a wide smile that matched my son's grin. I climbed the path to greet her, aware of the weight of my gun for the first time in days. I managed to overcome the automatic urge to touch the Colt. I'd gotten used to it and so would the Grandmother. Her eyes drifted back to my face as I topped the path. "Welcome, Lauren Maxwell."

After returning her greeting, I surveyed the camp. Dozens of filleted fish hung from the drying racks. Flesh tones ranged from blush to bronze but uniformity reigned in the deep cuts scoring each fillet. A curl of smoke rose from the small shack where other fillets underwent a smoke cure. A blue plastic tarp lashed to a crude frame shaded the worktable piled with another half-dozen salmon awaiting the Grandmother's ministrations.

I lifted a hand toward the worktable. "Would you show me how to clean a fish?"

Sarah Doyon hefted her curved fish knife and sliced three times, removing the head, tail, and fins from the salmon. Those bits she slopped into a plastic bucket. "Boil later for dogs."

Another deft move split the fish lengthwise, freeing the skeleton, which she pried out and tossed into yet another bucket along with the fish innards. "Bones in the river return the fish to life and to my wheel."

To the *Dene,* the cycles of nature reflect a great circle within which all life revolves. Goose feathers thrown into the river once again become birds, just as the fish bones return to life as the salmon of another summer. Hunters are careful to remove any bones from forest paths because that would inhibit the animal's rebirth and in time endanger

Elizabeth Quinn

the *Dene*'s survival as game dwindled. In their
world, close ties exist between people and nature.
Threading the eyes of a hawk onto a parka prevents
snow blindness, a large raven feather tied into a
child's hair makes the runner swift, and those who
eat of porcupine heart gain a share of the creature's
great courage.

The Grandmother laid out the gutted fish, leaving a narrow band of skin to hold the fillets
together, and then scored each deeply, allowing for
maximum air circulation on the drying rack. I
estimated the cleaning took no more than a minute
and wondered if Jake had mastered this task.

In answer to my question, the Grandmother
shrugged. "Men are not good for cutting fish."

I bristled at the news. "You mean Jake has been
goofing off instead of helping you?"

She reached for another salmon. "He is my
biggest help, that son you have, Lauren Maxwell."
Whack, whack, whack—head, tail, fins. "Not once
do I ask chop wood, get water, bring fish. What
Jake sees, he does."

Words to warm any mother's heart. My little
man. I couldn't help smiling.

He topped the path right then, shouldering my
pack and toting another fat salmon. "More work
for you, Sarah." He spilled the fish onto her table
and grinned when he noticed my outrage at his use
of the Grandmother's name. "Relax, Mom. Sarah
likes me using her name. Nobody else does. Not for
years and years."

He headed toward the cabin. The Grandmother

110

trailed him with brown eyes warm with affection.
"A fine son you have, Lauren Maxwell." She
turned back to me. "You see Belle at hospital?"

That question gave me the opening to return the
favor she'd done me by praising Jake. If her praise
warmed my heart, the Grandmother's own heart
would absolutely blaze when she learned of my
certainty that Belle had—and would—survive. I
described the machinery in the ICU, explaining
how the electronic blips matched Belle's heart-
beats. And then I told her about the rhythmic
squeeze that matched those electronic beats. "A
deep peace came over me then. I knew that Belle
was still in there. And I knew that she would pull
through."

The Grandmother laid aside her curved fish
knife. "So Belle dreams and cures herself." A smile
ghosted across her lips. "She may return to this
world a wise one."

"A wise one?" I frowned at her. Dreams? Wisdom? Both often derived from the spirit world. "As
some sort of shaman? How could that be?"

"Spirits come to those who die. And stay with
those who return to life." She reached for her knife
again. "Those who cure themselves can cure others."

Jake heard that last exchange as he returned
from dropping my pack in one of the cabins. "You
mean Belle's going to be a medicine man? Yip-
pee!" He gave the Grandmother's shoulder a gentle
pat. "She'll get everything back to normal, Sarah.
You'll see."

"Excuse me?" I must admit to feeling a bit miffed, almost an intruder. I wanted them to be friends, yes. But I hated being left out. Especially when recent abnormalities included the attempted murder of my friend. "What exactly isn't normal around here?"

"Everything!" Jake raised waving hands to shoulder height. "Animals aren't supposed to come to the villages. Not since the distant time. Or ravens, either. Without a shaman to keep things in balance, the whole world gets out of whack, Mom."

I glanced at the Grandmother, whose eyes gleamed at my son's recitation. He needed no further encouragement. "You see, I'm learning *Dene* ways from Sarah. She's been teaching me lots of stuff."

I smiled at his enthusiasm. "Like what?"

"Like what to have in your fire bag." He pulled aside the collar of his flannel shirt, revealing a small leather pouch hanging by a thong around his neck. "And how to track animals by following raven. And what to do when you see a bear. And fishing. And all the stories. I mean, lots and lots of stories, Mom. They're pretty cool."

I decided to impress my kid. "Stories about *Tsa-o-sha* and the rest of the gang?"

Impressed is not the word Jake used. "Awesome, Mom." His eyes danced with pleasure and pride. "You know about *Tsa-o-sha!* That's awesome."

I beamed back at him. Earning the pride of your child is a special joy. And a special responsibility. For once, I felt equal to the task of living up to

Jake's expectations. I must have been doing something right. This awesome kid was my son, after all.

"And that's not all I'm learning, Mom." He dug his hands into the front pockets of his jeans and came up with two shards of rock. "I met this guy over at the boneyards. He's letting me help with the dig. And he said I could keep these points that I found."

Points are what we tenderfeet used to call arrowheads. The ones Jake placed in my hand weren't whole. One point showed a definite notch at the base of the blade, but the other side of the point had broken off, notch included. The other point might have passed as a chip of rock to the untrained eye. I was definitely an amateur in things archaeological, but I'd seen enough points to recognize the primitive handiwork in the smooth flaking of rock. "You found these yourself?"

"You bet!" Jake grinned down at the artifacts in my hand. "And after Raphael took his pictures, he said I could keep 'em."

I closed my hand over Jake's points. "Who is Raphael?"

Jake held up a hushing hand. For a minute, I heard nothing except buzzing insects and whispering river. Then the high-pitched whine of an engine wafted over the Doyon fish camp.

My son danced from foot to foot. "Raphael's the guy in charge of the dig. That's him now."

An icy fog smothered the warm glow in my chest. One of the bone people. Maybe even the bone doctor himself! "He's coming here? Now?"

"Yup. That's him." Jake darted for the path to the beach and called over his shoulder. "Come on."

The Grandmother seemed unconcerned. She nodded her approval and waved me toward the beach. "Go now. I come."

I overcame my reluctance and followed my son. Maybe I was overreacting. Maybe it was all my imagination. I didn't actually know that the fellow at the Tanana post office was part of the archaeological expedition. And for that matter, I didn't have any real reason to suspect the bone people of involvement in the attack on Belle. The fact that the wolf pelt came from the Nowitna Refuge could be a simple matter of coincidence.

I paused at the edge of the bench and looked down at the beach below. A second boat had joined the Doyon skiff on the narrow strip of sand. And a man had joined my son on the path leading up the bench to the Doyon fish camp.

A man with a good haircut. Who else?

14

Manners maketh man. Max often quoted his old prep school motto during our frequent rehashes of the nature versus nurture debate. My late husband thought that the ability to understand an opponent's point of view and to feel an enemy's pain were the hallmarks of our humanity. "Any two idiots can make a fight," he said, "but it takes brains to get along." For Max, manners were the grease that kept the civilized wheel from squeaking. Turned out that Raphael Tocco certainly would have met with his approval.

He came at me up that path with hand outstretched. "I'd hoped to make your acquaintance earlier this afternoon at the village post office. I trust my clumsy attempt didn't interfere too much with your telephone call?"

Talk about smooth. His bright blue eyes sparkled

with humor, but his words and tone had just the right blend of polished sincerity. I allowed him to take my hand as I gave the expected reply. "Not at all."

His lean, strong hand gave mine a brisk, no-nonsense shake. That good haircut tamed a thick, dark mane that showed not a hint of gray. I'd expected a man near my own age or at least midthirties, but Raphael Tocco came up a decade short. I decided to test his good manners on exactly that point. "You seem awfully young to be heading up a dig."

His cheeks flushed pink. "I don't head up the dig, Mrs. Maxwell." He ducked his head like a skittish cub. "Preston Waite is the man in charge. I'm just his teaching assistant."

Raphael Tocco's blush disarmed me. That plus his humility. Many of today's graduate students adopt an attitude of bristling arrogance. This kid refreshed me. And his next words about finished me off.

"Jake told me that you'll be studying the remnant Beringian steppe vegetation in the Nowitna refuge." Another duck of the head. "I had hoped you might let me tag along? I'm sure everything I learn will be very useful to my own studies."

Sometimes flattery works. A blush of my own crept up my neck and, to cover my embarrassment, I stuck out my hand again. "Deal."

All this time, Jake had hung back from our exchange, an eager observer but in no way a participant. Now he bounced forward and touched

Raphael's elbow. "Tell her what you said when I asked about your job."

"You would bring that up, Maxwell." He smiled down at my son with true affection and then turned to me, rolling his eyes. "I told Jake that I had a sissy job to match my sissy name."

That was the knockout punch. I was down for the count, and the bout went to Raphael Tocco. For the rest of the evening, my suspicions joined me on the mat—out cold.

Jake led the way to the fire pit he'd constructed near the largest cabin, now containing a teepee of dry fuel seasoned with green kindling to keep the bugs away. I seated myself on one of the rounds of wood half-circled around the fire facing south. The sun hung low in the west, dipping toward setting just after 10 P.M. The river slid by, slow and easy. Sarah Doyon came out of the large cabin carrying a tray laden with tea and pilot bread and chocolate bars. Raphael Tocco helped her settle the refreshments and then chose a round of wood next to mine. After a quick glance to confirm the attendance of all his guests, my son struck a match against a rock and lit the fire. Flames licked up the teepee of wood, sending a shower of sparks into the darkening sky.

I leaned toward the fire's warmth and tossed a question to the young scientist seated at my side. "What exactly do you want with my Beringian remnants?"

"Not a new location for a dig." He looked at me gravely. "Rest assured that Preston Waite considers that remnant steppe as sacred ground. Living fossils, actually. Survivors of the Upper Paleolithic still living thirty thousand years later." A deep sigh escaped him. "You can't know how I envy you your job."

"But why?" I'd always assumed that other scientists chose their fields for the same reason I had chosen biology—because all other disciplines seemed utterly dull in comparison. Didn't every scientist love her field to the exclusion of all others? "Your work must be fascinating."

"Fascinating." He made it sound anything but. "And dead. Archaeology is the science of the dead. Even the most magnificent finds of primitive man are literally from the grave. All properly prepared and laid out in burial. Of living man, we have no trace."

He turned to me, eyes bright in the firelight. "But you have the living earth of Beringia. Earth he might have walked across. Steppes he might have hunted over."

"Well, not exactly." I lifted my shoulders into a shrug. "Those remnants are nothing more than descendants of the Upper Paleolithic steppe. No living thing has ever survived thirty thousand years. And you of all people should know that primitive man walked over just about every inch of the planet."

Sarah Doyon spared Raphael Tocco the need to reply by pouring out the tea. She handed him a cracked mug along with a round biscuit of pilot bread. "You like chocolate, too?"

For long minutes, we munched and sipped and let the chocolate melt over our tongues. The sun had dipped below the western edge of the world, painting the sky the same brilliant bronze as the flesh of freshly caught salmon. Bats swooped over the Yukon, which whispered by, a gleam of silver. Far over our heads the stars winked on, one by one. Jake fed fresh fuel into the fire, sending up another shower of sparks that drew all eyes. The Grandmother stared at the sky overhead. "Wind coming. See those stars swaying?"

Swaying or twinkling, both describe the same phenomenon. The effect is caused by the increase in atmospheric moisture that signals an approaching storm. Jake leaned toward the Grandmother, asking something about the stars. And Raphael Tocco leaned toward me. "On a night like this, I have no difficulty placing myself in that ancient world."

I smiled encouragement. "Tell me about it."

"The land lay beneath towering sheets of ice which dried up the seas." He spread his hands. "Two continental glaciers more than a mile high spreading from the east and from the west. Only this river valley remained free of perpetual winter. This river valley provided the only refuge from the ice."

I snagged a pebble from the ground at my feet, rolling its warmth between my palms. "Refuge sounds like a bit of an overstatement."

"Not at all." He shook his head. "Refuge is the exact word. This valley provided refuge to bison, musk ox, caribou, mammoth, even lions. And to man."

His eyes glittered in the firelight. "There was no Bering Sea. There was no Bering Strait. There was only Beringia, an island of earth amid all of that ice. The mammoths crossed over. And so did man."

The pebble in my hand had cooled. I tossed it into the fire. "And is your theory that man followed the animals across the land bridge?"

"Perhaps." Raphael Tocco lifted his eyes toward the stars swaying over our heads. "Or perhaps he just followed the stars. Do you believe in destiny?"

I swallowed the urge to laugh with delight. Dreamers are such sweet pleasure, even in science. "I believe in reason. And reason says that primitive man would have had a tough time surviving this far north in the Upper Paleolithic."

He lowered his head and looked at me. "Why do you say that?"

"Because of the threshold technology required for survival." I ticked off the points on one hand. "Adequate clothing, adequate shelter, adequate food gathering and winter storage, a means of moving over snow and cold water. The northern limit seems to be about sixty degrees latitude. Beyond that, there would be few woody materials for shelter or fuel or tools."

"Ever been to the Old Crow basin in the Yukon Territory?" I shook my head, and he sat back, crossing an ankle over a knee and holding it in place with laced fingers. "The bars contain thousands of fossilized bones, teeth, tusks, and antlers. You literally cannot take a step without landing on a fossil bone."

I nodded. Another boneyard, like the one he was digging just upriver. As late as the early seventies the Nowitna's banks contained similar deposits. "What's your point?"

"For years, the skeptics have pointed out the dearth of wood for fires. And the lack of stone tools." He took a deep breath and let it out slowly. "But what if primitive man eschewed stone tools in favor of bone tools? And what if he burned the bone he had in place of the wood he lacked?"

Zzzing! One small question for Lauren, one giant leap for science! My ears hummed with excitement. A little change in perspective can make all the difference in the world. In that instant, Raphael Tocco's imagination had started making sense. Which is exactly what I said.

Another bashful duck of the head. "I'd love to claim that theory as my own, but I can't." A hush came over his voice. "That honor belongs to Preston Waite. Beringia is his life's work."

Sounds corny, I know, but his reverence touched me. In every scientist's life, there is one great teacher who leads and guides and prods the novice toward whatever wisdom can eventually be claimed. My great teacher was a munchkin of a biologist with a gray bun and a deceptively sweet manner, who held tenure at SUNY Buffalo. Although she died several years ago, Professor Isaacs still inhabits my dreams, and I still wake up sweating whenever she asks me a question that leaves me stumped.

Jake heard Raphael's last words and chimed right in. "Dr. Waite's pretty old, Mom. But he's okay. He asked us to dinner tomorrow night."

I grinned at my son across the campfire. "And what did we answer?"

"You bet." Jake grinned back at me. "Maybe he'll let you look for points, too!"

Points or no, I wouldn't complain. One thing all novice scientists learn early on: Never pass up a chance to spend time with a great teacher. Quite simply, their like may never cross your path again.

15

The wind that swayed the stars blew a stormy morning over the Doyon fish camp. The Grandmother woke at the first patter of rain, rousing Jake when she slipped out the door. From the warm and drowsy recesses of my sleeping bag in the tiny loft above the kitchen, I heard them go and considered following. Tarps had to be thrown over how many drying racks? Six sounded right. A milky morning light filled my cozy nook, and the storm beat gently against the tin roof hanging three feet above my pillow. Which aphorism to follow—"Too many cooks spoil the broth," or "The more the merrier"? Before I had an answer, the rain lulled me back to sleep.

Sleeping in on foul days is one of my favorite bush traditions. Let those fat salmon stay in the fish trap a few hours longer. Make that fresh water in the bucket last another meal or two. Postpone the morning trip to the outhouse until just a little bit later. Instead, snuggle down into the warmth of the nest and experience the ultimate rest that comes with wilderness repose. Not even the twitter of birds disturbs a foul weather morning in the bush.

But rest doesn't come easy to a worried mind. Stray anxieties hovered around the edges of my sleep and darted like angry wraiths into my dreams. Belle Doyon, leading with vigorous steps on our recent backcountry trek until she stopped and turned a bruised and battered face to me. Fabian Lavigne, rebuilding his engine with agile fingers that suddenly sprouted fur to match the thick wolf ruff replacing his beard. Eleanor Demissov, opening with the utmost tenderness the boxes filled with ancestors until discovering in one her own fleshed-over skull. Raphael Tocco, charming in his boyish enthusiasm until the excited glitter in his blue eyes turned into a menacing gleam. And my own dear Jake, every beloved inch of him vibrant with life as he walked toward some dread horror that crouched in the forest just beyond our sight. I opened my mouth to warn him but no sound emerged. I reached out my hand to stop him but no movement occurred. I stood frozen, silent, and my mind screamed his name. Jake . . . Jake . . .

"Mom?" A gentle nudge against my shoulder. "Wake up, Mom."

And there he was, my own dear Jake, perched on

the ladder to the loft and peering at me with solemn brown eyes. I reached for him. "I had an awful dream."

He allowed his head to be pulled next to mine and endured my nuzzling of his firm yet soft cheek. "Dreams aren't awful and dreams aren't wonderful, Mom." He reared back to echo my own soothing words from his nightmare years. "Dreams are just dreams."

Maybe so, but mine unsettled the rest of my day. Rain pounded down throughout the breakfast that I ate without really tasting. The storm slackened as I leafed through a shelf of paperbacks, reading a page here and another there. I couldn't get interested in the news on Alaska Public Radio or the cutthroat checkers match between Jake and the Grandmother. The sun appeared just past noon, a hot August sun that set everything steaming and left me sticky from the mugginess. The tarps came off of the fish racks and the salmon came in from the pen beneath the fish wheel. Then the Grandmother brought out her fish knife and went happily to her seasonal task while I dragged Jake off on a hike. But even an exhausting forced march would not have settled my nerves. What I wanted to be doing was catching Belle's attacker, and that task had to wait at least until suppertime. When at last the hour arrived for our departure to our dinner date at the archaeological dig, I was on red alert, eager to shoot first and ask questions later. The evening seemed certain to end in disaster.

Jake ferried us upstream and across the river,

angling toward shore when we approached the high silt bluffs known as the Palisades. I'd noticed the beachhead on my barge trip downriver. Very tidy and un-Alaskan, especially the flashy new motorized raft pulled up on the shore that looked like something out of a James Bond movie or a Greenpeace fund-raising appeal. After tying up alongside, we made our way up the steep path to the very un-Alaskan bush camp of Dr. Preston Waite.

Imagine combining Cecil B. DeMille's love of spectacle with Donald Trump's love of luxury. Think *Out of Africa* meets *White Fang*. A half dozen of the huge and impractical canvas tents that went out with the Civil War formed the perimeter of Camp Waite. Each boasted a roofed front area that housed small tables and chairs, including one with a monster recliner that undoubtedly belonged to the great man himself. A sideless mess tent anchored one end of the camp while a buttoned-down number with a sign warning AUTHORIZED EMPLOYEES ONLY anchored the other. A couple of fresh-faced young women scurried around the mess tent and camp kitchen, laying out place settings and stirring pots, and a pair of clean-cut young men loitered purposefully near the head man's tent. The only thing needed to complete the scene was a couple of bearers shouting "bwana." Big-time science hadn't changed. And nobody'd ever said a great teacher can't be a real jerk.

The flap of the head man's tent opened and out stepped a skinny old man with a bushy halo of white hair à la Dr. Zorba. He spotted us standing in the shadow of a spruce and stepped toward us. "Welcome. Welcome."

The unmoving young men in his wake looked around in confusion. He shot them a baleful glance. "Idiots. My guests have arrived. Look there."

And then the entire camp came alive. The clean-cut young men darted to their great teacher's side. One fresh-faced young woman took drink orders while another offered a succession of munchies. Raphael Tocco appeared from somewhere to oil the squeaks with his charming manners. And Dr. Preston Waite, the great man himself, very briefly displayed—and just as quickly disguised—extreme annoyance at discovering the Grandmother among those who'd come to dinner. A native, of all people!

Jake also noticed his displeasure and hissed a warning in my ear. "I told you he was old."

I hissed right back. "Since when does advanced age automatically equal bigotry?"

When my son came back with a good imitation of my own trademark glare, I relented. No need to embarrass him or the Grandmother, or myself. Undoubtedly some social arbiter has drawn up a list of tips for making the best of a bad situation, but at Camp Waite deep in Alaska's bush, I had to wing it on nothing more than my mother's all-purpose advice for every conceivable social situation: Give others a chance to talk about themselves. As we sipped our cocktails, the clean-cut

young man named Kim told me that his archaeological passion dated from his adolescent hobby of
collecting obsidian points from the tule marshes of
northern California. While we savored a first
course of smoked Yukon salmon, the fresh-faced
young woman named Marcia explained how she
discovered her future profession when a minor
hurricane uncovered the skeleton of a Spanish brig
near her home on a Florida key. During our old-
style, high-style entrée of fillet mignon, Dr. Preston
Waite turned the tables on me by asking a raft of
questions, the most pointed professional vetting
I've ever endured. And after we'd gobbled up the
last of our blueberry cheesecake, Raphael Tocco
brought the conversation back to our common
purpose: Upper Paleolithic relics, fossil or living.
He directed his first words to his teacher. "Dr.
Maxwell intends to survey the Nowitna for remnants of the Beringian steppe."

Preston Waite theatrically signaled his surprise
by lifting his eyebrows. "Surely that work has been
done."

"That's what the feds claim, but I'm guessing the
job was strictly hit or miss. As usual." My voice
sounded too sharp. I tried for modulation. "The
Wild America Society is concerned mostly with
those areas near the river which are likely to receive
the most foot traffic. Especially the south slopes
above benchlands near Boney Creek. I hear that's
an agate-hunter's heaven."

His eyes clouded for a moment and then refocused on me. "Young Tocco here tells me you

actually arrived in the village on the plane that carried the Smithsonian artifacts?"

The switch of topics left me playing catch-up. "Yes. I did."

Jake leaned forward and joined in, his voice an adolescent chime. "We both did."

The old man ignored my son. "Shocking decision." His frown left deep grooves on his withered cheeks. "Disgraceful. Set the field back a hundred years."

"But nobody even looked at the ancestors until the village asked for them back." Jake quivered with all the strident certainty of youth. "And they weren't just artifacts. They were family."

Ever so slowly, Preston Waite turned his head toward my son and gave him a scornful look that shouted "seen but not heard." Evidently, the old man expected me to provide the sound track. A few years earlier, I might have. Back then, I still found myself embarrassed by Jake's habit of addressing adults as equals. Most adults expect deference from children, but few receive that from my son. After about thirty seconds had passed without the expected reprimand, the great teacher turned his attention back to me, eyebrows again theatrically raised.

"Jake's right, of course. That's one thing science has absolutely proved. We're all part of the same family." I gave the old man my sweetest smile. "The human family."

And then I gathered up two of my dearest relations and took them home.

16

The battered aluminum sled skimmed down the wide river, slicing through the occasional chop thrown up by a stray breeze. From the start of our trip I studied the water ahead, looking for the wrinkles and whorls that could be trouble. Meaning a rock in the channel, a log floating just under the surface, a shifting bar of gravel. Running into, over, or onto any of those obstructions could be very bad trouble on a river as swift and cold as the Yukon. Not that I didn't trust my son's ability to read the water. Jake grew up running rivers and can thread a raft through a maze of whitewater. But motorboats demand skills I wasn't certain that he'd mastered.

Jake throttled back, slowing the boat. "How about that island over there?" He pointed to a wooded one near the southern bank. "Looks interesting."

To the uninitiated, Jake's island wouldn't appear any more interesting than the many others we'd passed. Yet I knew immediately what attracted him. Water seeped down one side of the stony beach. Maybe a spring? A jumble of huge boulders formed a high promontory. Maybe a cave?

I cupped my hands to keep the breeze from snatching away my words. "Looks good, sweetie. And I'm starving."

Jake made a preliminary exploration while I dug our lunch out of my day pack. PB&J sandwiches, granola bars, oranges, a bag of chocolate kisses, and hot cocoa—not exactly a gourmet spread, but even the most pedestrian food tastes marvelous when eaten outdoors. Yesterday's rain had washed the air to a sparkling clarity and swept the sky to a dazzling brilliance. The forest across the river looked like a rising crescendo, with the palette of each new ridge dominated by a different shade of green. The brightness of the river bottom's poplars and white birch gave way to the darker, richer spruce before peaking in the yellowing hues of sparse willow and alder at the treeline.

I'd feasted on that beauty and one sandwich by the time my son returned, carrying a fresh-cut switch of spruce in one hand. After downing two sandwiches, two granola bars, an orange, and several hearty swigs of hot cocoa, Jake brought out his jackknife and whittled while I took my ease against a day-pack pillow and sucked on a chocolate kiss. After a few minutes of companionable silence, he lobbed me a real hand grenade of a question. "Mom? Do you think I'll ever be a real Alaskan?"

In Alaska, queries like that contain more explosive potential than a gold miner's annual supply of TNT. Some argue that true Alaskans are born, some contend that true Alaskans are made, and never the twain shall meet. In answering, I adopted a strategy that had worked for me in the past: play dumb and stall for time.

"I don't know what you mean, honey." I adjusted the brim of my ball cap to shade out the sun. "You were born right here. In Anchorage."

"Yeah. Yeah." His words dripped scorn. "In a hospital."

"Damn right. With a vet for your Dad and a lab rat for your Mom, where else could it happen?"

He had the good grace to chuckle but couldn't sustain the laughter. Meaning this was serious stuff so I better listen up. "What I mean is . . . if you've never wintered over out here, can you be a real Alaskan?"

Trust a kid to cut through the BS and get right to the heart of the matter. The crux of the argument, indeed. Are those of us who winter in Anchorage— with our heat pumps and hot running water and municipally plowed streets and high-culture diversions imported from the Lower 48—are we the real Alaskans? Or are those who winter in the bush— with their snow machines and satellite receivers and shares of stock in regional corporations and airborne high school sports rivalries—are they the real Alaskans?

I rolled onto my side and propped myself on an elbow before answering. "I don't know that there's one sure test of a real Alaskan. But I do know that Alaskans get tested. Some by choice, some by circumstance, but all of us are tested in one way or another."

He slipped the blade of his knife under the spruce bark and peeled it off with one smooth motion. "You and Dad wintered over out here one year."

"Once. But not out here, Jake." I lifted an arm and pointed to the northwest. "Out there. Way out there and way up there at Point Hope. And I never would have made it without your father."

He slid his knife under the last strip of bark and then rolled the spruce switch between his fingers. "How come?"

"The darkness." I couldn't contain a shiver. "The cold. Sometimes our stove actually glowed red. And I never knew before that winter just how much I need the sun."

"That why we go to Hawaii every year?" He pulled one of the points from his jeans pocket and threw me a grin. "Not that I mind or anything. What did you do up there?"

Made love, mostly, although I couldn't tell him that. "We studied polar bears." But if I didn't tell Jake the facts of life, who would? "And we were young and in love. Which generated a lot of heat and a lot of light."

"Some test." He gave me a crooked smile. "What was the hardest one?"

Finally, a question whose answer came easily. "Getting out of bed the day I woke up and knew that I'd never see your dad again."

Jake blinked hard a few times. I reached across the beach and gave his leg a quick squeeze. "How about you?"

He bit his lower lip, as much from concentrating on fitting his point onto his arrow as from worrying over my question. "Same thing, I guess. And flying with Travis after Dad crashed."

"You're kidding." I elbowed myself erect. "You never said a word. You never acted scared."

Jake studied the point on his arrow and then shifted his gaze to me. "Letting it show doesn't make it any better, Mom. Sometimes you just do what you've got to do."

Coming from an adult, that statement was often just words. Coming from a child, the same words carried a weight of wisdom. A few years ago, I realized that the earth's children are the greatest untapped resource left on the planet. Along with that realization came the determination that I, for one, intended to start listening to them.

Not much later, we gathered our life jackets and gear into the boat and headed back upstream to the Doyon fish camp. The breeze at our backs left me deaf to everything but the whine of the outboard motor. That same upstream breeze at once raised a low chop and pushed the sled over the waves with an uncomfortable bouncing motion. I gestured toward the slack water running down the northern bank. Jake angled the sled in that direction.

Just before we reached the eddy, an insect buzzed loudly in my ear. I swatted one hand. Then came a sharp tug from behind and I went ass over teakettle into the bottom of the boat.

I landed sprawled on my back in gasoline-fouled bilge water with my legs hooked over my seat. Water spurted in from both sides of the boat, two nice round streams that might have come from a hose. What in hell did we hit? And what about Jake?

I started to raise myself up, but my hair caught on something. I reached to free myself. My hand found another. Jake!

I craned my head around. He lay on the floor, spread-eagled at an awkward angle, one hand wrapped around my own and the other gripping the outboard's control arm.

Again I moved to rise. Again he held me down. "Stay down, Mom. He's still shooting."

Shooting? That stiffened me. Then a weird noise—*za-pop*—that drew Jake's eyes beyond me. I shifted my own and discovered two new streams of water now filling the boat.

Filling the boat! Sinking the boat!

I jerked back to face Jake, sloshing my hair through deepening water. "Are you okay?"

He gave me a tiny nod. "Yeah. But we're going in, Mom." Never had his eyes been wider or rounder. "I'm still on my heading, but the holes are slowing us down. We'll never make it now."

I gave his hand a sharp squeeze. "We'll make it."

Water splashed over my shoulders. Numbing cold water. How long before hypothermia immobilized us? Water poured in from four good-size holes. How long before our life jackets lifted us into the range of the sniper's sight?

I focused on Jake again. "We've got to stay low. Take off your life jacket."

He looked at me without blinking. "But we'll drown."

Already he'd lifted his head to raise his face out of the water. Already I'd stretched my neck so I could breathe. "What about going over the side?"

Jake's frown screwed up his face. "Without life jackets, we'll drown. But floating, he'll shoot us."

Ka-wang!

Another shot careened off the heavier rolled metal of the sled's gunwale. The stark impossibility of our survival struck me dumb. My racing mind turned sluggish, filling with despair. Maybe we weren't going to make it after all.

Then Jake yanked his hand from mine. "I know!"

His hand snaked under the water and then surfaced, grasped around the hose of the bilge pump. "We'll breathe through this. Like *Tsa-o-sha*. Take it. And get out of your life jacket."

I took the plastic hose and his jackknife, too. *Tsa-o-sha* hid from bear at the bottom of a pond by breathing through a reed! If we could stay hidden in the bottom of the boat until it sank, the sniper might think he'd gotten us.

I cut the hose into equal lengths and handed one back to my son. "Good thinking."

"It'll be okay, Mom." He managed a half-smile. "You'll see."

I managed one bit of genius of my own, remembering to use the carabiner on my day pack to clip our supplies onto my gun belt. Then I gripped one end of the makeshift breathing tube with my teeth and laced my fingers through Jake's. And after gathering my courage, I let the icy Yukon waters close over my face.

17

Cold. So cold. The extremities went first. The toes seized up, immovable. The feet grew dense and heavy, like rocks. The hands grew hollow and brittle, like glass. Except where my fingers twined with Jake's fingers. His touch became my focal point. As our world withered away, the touch of Jake's hand became my still point at the center of the universe.

I closed my eyes, unable to bear the shimmer of light floating just out of reach. The vibration of the aluminum boat told me the sled still plowed the Yukon water, furrowing ever deeper. Definitely into the eddy now. And nearing shore. But how near?

The air of the breathing tube came oiled and burning to my tongue, a bitter blessing. My jaws throbbed from the effort of anchoring the plastic hose with my teeth. An involuntary shiver started to build deep inside dulled muscles. I flattened my tongue across the hose, a fleshy plug that could not hold the river back for long.

A shudder beneath my shoulders. Then a sudden life-giving squeeze from Jake's hand. I opened my eyes and water billowed as the boat fell away. The squared-off bow drifted toward us and then slipped into the green murk below.

Buoyed by the air in our lungs, Jake and I floated toward the surface, hands still twined. I clawed the water with my free hand, desperate to dig us deeper, slowed by my sluggish arm. Jake's free arm worked better than mine, and his legs propelled us toward shore with a slow, steady flutter kick.

And then my lower back scraped bottom. I spit the hose from my mouth and lifted my face toward the air, allowing only my nose and mouth and eyes above the surface as my feet and legs settled under me. At the edge of my water-rimmed vision, a thick shag of grass thatched a muddy bank topped by poplars.

Next to me, Jake's face broke the surface and he sucked air. I squeezed his hand to catch his attention. "Can you hear me?"

The water in my ears flattened my words and Jake's reply. "I hear you, Mom."

Another squeeze, a hard one that I held for emphasis. "Catch your breath. Then get to those poplars. Fast."

He squeezed back, then let go of my hand. A

splash, a scramble, and he burst from the river, slopping muddy water across my face.

I started counting. Cold. No problem lasting to ten. So cold. Twenty was harder. Too cold. Thirty turned out to be my limit.

With all the strength left in me, I sprang out of my crouch, diving toward the muddy bank with outstretched arms, crawling through the thick grass with pumping knees, scrabbling into the shade of the poplar thicket to find my son hunkered down among the saplings. My Jake. My dripping, grinning, sobbing, darling boy.

I slung an arm around his shoulders and pulled him close. "We have to get out of here. Can you make it?"

Honking, sniffing, gasping, and shivering, he nodded. That bucked me up enough to start my search. I threaded between the poplars, heading away from the river, looking for the right spot to regroup. I needed thick woods most definitely. High ground if possible. And not too far.

The spot we lucked onto proved perfect, with plenty of downed wood for a fire. I unclipped the sodden day pack from my gun belt and groped inside, searching for lighter and fire starter, while Jake gathered fuel. As my hand closed around the tube of fire ribbon, I realized that Jake had other ideas for starting a fire. He'd unfastened the fire bag from his neck and pulled out his flint and pyrite. And he started shaving curls of wood into a little pile, mixing the shavings with *Fomes igniarius,* a birch fungus the *Dene* use as tinder.

One squirt of starter gel touched off by my never-fail lighter would produce a blazing fire in an instant. But our need to get dry and warm could be postponed for a little while. I let go of the tube of starter and felt for the space blanket instead. Now that we were out of the river, we weren't in immediate danger of hypothermia. And my son deserved a chance to pass this test. The whole point of summering in fish camp was to rebuild the boy's self-esteem. The Grandmother had provided the building blocks. Mastering this moment could supply the cement necessary to complete the job.

Jake struck a spark into the little pile of shavings and fungus and drew a tiny corkscrew of smoke as a reward. At the first flicker, he began slowly feeding the fire. Slowly, slowly, adding just twigs until the flicker became a flame. Then he offered larger pieces, sticks the diameter of his thumb. When the flame multiplied into tongues of fire licking over the sticks from all directions, he carefully tented a couple of small logs over the fire, rocked back onto his heels and gave me a triumphant smile.

"Nice work, Jake." I tossed him the Mylar space blanket. "Let's get out of these wet things and dry off."

Before undressing, I studied the rising smoke, gratified to see that the thick canopy of branches overhead strained the column into a diffuse cloud. Our sniper would have trouble pinpointing the source. I unbuckled my gun belt and laid it aside. When I reached for the buttons of my flannel shirt, I noticed that the .45 kept drawing my son's eyes. "What's wrong, honey? Does the gun bother you?"

He shook his head, eyes sliding away. Then he scooted closer to the fire and held up his jeans to dry. "Will it work when it's wet?"

Good question. And one I couldn't answer. I bunched up my flannel shirt, wringing out as much water as possible. Now that the adrenaline high had worn off, Jake might plunge into fear. Which had to be avoided. "I'm not sure if getting a gun wet is a problem. Maybe we better check."

I stood up to shuck off my own jeans and decided not to insist on peeling to bare naked. For a boy who never minded showing his bare butt, my son had grown surprisingly modest, especially around Mom. Soggy undies certainly wouldn't bring on hypothermia. Not with Jake's roaring fire and my space blanket to create a cocoon of warm air.

Jake changed his jeans to his other hand and finally gave me a nod, one firm and definite nod. "We should, Mom. In case he's still out there. I mean, we may need it."

"Let's hope not." I folded into a crouch and laid the gun belt across my knees, taking it slow to prove my competence and give him time to get used to his gun-toting mama. "If this gun fires, the sound could help him figure out where we are."

I pulled the Colt out of the holster and jacked out the cartridge. "Definitely wet. Of course, firing also shows him we're armed. And I think letting him know we can shoot back is more important than worrying about him locating us."

I snapped the cartridge back in place. "What do you think?"

Jake's arm sagged under the weight of his jeans, and he shivered, huddling closer to the fire. "Try it."

"Only if you'll get under this space blanket." I snagged the reflecting blanket with one hand, shook out the folds, and then draped it over one of Jake's shoulders. "And remember, this thing is loud."

He shawled the Mylar blanket around himself and nodded.

I moved a couple of yards away and assumed the position: palms clapped, left foot forward, right arm straight, and left arm ready to bend. Then I threw Jake a promise that I hoped I could keep. "Watch the bottom branch of that spruce."

I sighted carefully, controlled my breathing, and squeezed the trigger. *BLAM!* The Colt bucked against my hand, leaving one less branch on the spruce.

The explosive clap made Jake cringe, but not for long. He turned to me with wide eyes. "Wow! Do it again!"

"No way." I came back to the fire and slid the .45 back into the holster. "We've already proved it works and let that jerk know that we are armed and dangerous." I slid the belt around my bare midriff and buckled it on. "But just in case he doesn't care, firing again would make us lots easier to find."

A rush of tears left my son's eyes shimmering,

but he blinked them back. "Who's after us, Mom? And why?"

"Why, I can't tell you." I held my jeans near the fire, close enough to start them steaming and sizzling, and leveled my gaze onto Jake. "But I think it's probably the same person who shot Belle. And I'm pretty sure it's somebody from the dig."

Jake opened his mouth to reply but no words came out. His lips trembled for an instant, and when the tears finally spilled he looked away.

I didn't press the point. Not yet. The wet leather of the gun belt felt slick and clammy against my skin, a sensation somehow queasy and comforting at the same time. Funny that my son assumed that our attacker was a man. I'd made the same mistake not long before and almost paid with my life. Throughout nature, the female is just as deadly as the male. But this time my gut told me Jake was right. I couldn't stretch my imagination far enough to make those cheerful coeds camped near the Palisades capable of mayhem. But imagining a gun in Raphael Tocco's hand didn't require even a tug. Remembering the fierce intensity that had glittered in his eyes one starlit night was all it took. That fellow cared enough to kill. At that moment, why didn't enter my equation. What mattered right then was who. Why could be answered later. Much later.

Jake stared at the fire with troubled eyes. The space blanket had slipped from his shoulders, and the knees of his jeans had started to singe.

I nudged his arm. "Your jeans are burning."

He jerked the pants away from the fire, muttering under his breath as he gave the knees a bunch of quick slaps. With Jake suitably distracted, the time had come to press my theory.

I kept my voice entirely neutral. "Your friend Raphael's the one who worries me. For a couple of reasons."

Jake missed a beat but kept on slapping his jeans. Meaning he shared my suspicion? Or at least was willing to hear me out.

"First reason is Raphael's interest in the Doyon fish camp, especially in light of Dr. Waite's bigotry." Forcing my son to choose between friends was cruel but necessary. "The professor obviously did not want the Grandmother at his table. Why would a devoted assistant disregard the old man's wishes?"

Jake laid the jeans aside, raised his shirt toward the fire, and offered a tentative defense of his new friend. "Maybe because Raphael isn't a jerk."

I reached for my own flannel shirt. "Maybe. But would you say he's ambitious?"

My son's eyes widened with outrage. "All of a sudden that's bad?"

"Not at all. But ambitious students don't ignore their teacher's prejudices." I shook out my shirt and lifted it toward the fire. "Remember, Jake. I've been there. I served my time as a Ph.D. grind."

When my son failed to respond, I pressed my advantage. "Plus Raphael Tocco is very mobile. He goes to town. He comes to fish camp. He has a motor raft at his disposal at all times."

"That doesn't make him a murderer." Jake's words carried more certainty than showed in his eyes. "It could be anybody, Mom. Why does it have to be Raphael?"

"Because of the wolf pelts the Grandmother found on her doorstep. The lab in Fairbanks says those wolves came from the Nowitna." For emphasis, I spit out each word individually. "Dr. Waite and his staff are the only group who've been at the refuge all summer."

Jake let the damp shirt fall onto his naked knees, oblivious to the sleeve trailing in the dirt. I gave him time to run the scenario through his mind and work the outrage out of his system. Which gave me time to start drafting my words of farewell. A few hours to get back to fish camp. Radioing Tanana for a boat would cost another hour or two. But Jake could make the last plane out tonight and be back in Anchorage before bedtime. Self-esteem boosted by survival today and out of harm's way tonight. So simple, so safe, and such swill. Life just doesn't deliver that kind of sweet dream.

"Maybe it's Raphael. And maybe not." Jake finally lifted his gaze from the fire and confronted me with sad but resolute eyes. "But we'll get him, Mom. We'll find out who, and then we'll get him."

That's how dreams turn into nightmares. You boost a kid's confidence only to find out he's ready to take on a killer. And too late, you realize that denying him the chance could cripple his self-esteem forever.

18

Jake hated my plan to trap Raphael Tocco and took small comfort in my marksmanship with the .45-caliber Colt automatic.

"Good against a tree is one thing, Mom." His voice vibrated with emotion. "Good against a guy that's shooting back is something else."

My son had a point, but I refused to concede. No way would I risk my twelve-year-old again. That's what he wanted—to tag along on the day of fieldwork I'd scheduled with Raphael Tocco, counting and cataloging the remnant Beringian steppe vegetation of the Nowitna drainage. Not a chance! But to preserve his precious male self-esteem, I had to short-circuit that burgeoning machismo with some other appeal. Reason? Definitely chancey, in light of Jake's raging testosterone. Guilt? Now there was a powerful tool for manipulation.

"Okay, Jake. Fine." The whipsaw in my whisper grabbed his attention. "Something goes wrong, and we'll both take a bullet in the base of the skull. Then who gets shot? Belle's already a vegetable, so I guess he'll take out the Grandmother next."

A dozen yards away, Sarah Doyon worked at her fish table, humming a little song as she sliced, split, and hung the day's catch of salmon. Jake's forehead creased and one hand chipped the bark of the round of wood on which he sat.

I leaned toward him across the dead ashes of the fire pit and set the hook. "When we don't return, she'll start wondering what happened. And pretty soon she'll start asking."

His gaze shifted, flickering over my face before returning to the old woman so happy in her work. A frown furrowed his cheeks as his fingers dug a canal through the spruce bark.

I sharpened my voice, honing that hook. "The first person she'll ask is Raphael Tocco. The first and the last. He'll take out that old lady without even breaking a sweat."

Jake's chin trembled but his eyes remained dry. Someday I'd have time to grieve for his lost innocence, but I didn't allow even primal sorrow to distract me that afternoon. If keeping Jake safe required armoring my maternal heart, I would be the coldest, hardest mother on the last frontier.

"Okay." The word whooshed out with a huge

sigh, and his head slumped. "What do you want me to do?"

"Thanks, Jake." I reached across and gave his knee a quick squeeze. "I knew I could count on you."

Through the afternoon and into the long twilight, we studied USGS survey maps of the Nowitna drainage. I hadn't been in that country for years and found myself dependent on Jake's recent explorations for up-to-date information. My son proved to have a good eye for detail, remembering such land features as morphology, botany, and orientation that helped target sites for my survey. Geomorphology demanded steep slopes or bluffs, botany required vegetation dominated by *Artemisia* species, and orientation dictated a south facing. By the time we rerolled the map, Jake had helped me pinpoint a half-dozen sites near Boney Creek that promised to be easy to reach and likely to hold relict vegetation of the Beringia Refugium.

In the hour before sunrise the next morning, I crept down from the loft to meet Raphael Tocco at first light. The Grandmother cracked an eye, but I laid hushing fingers against my lips to forestall conversation. She'd accepted the loss of her motor and boat with the practiced stoicism of all boreal peoples, and was too polite to ask an unwelcome question. No need to remind her to look after Jake. The elder's responsibility to the young is a given among the *Dene*.

Raphael Tocco arrived with the dawn, and the

wake of his motorized raft sent a ripple across the smooth, silvering Yukon water. He beached the raft and hopped out to offer me a hand getting in. "Jake's gone to the village this early? He must have the eyes of a falcon. I sure couldn't drive this raft in the dark."

I managed to stumble while climbing across the raft tube and took my time steadying myself. Let him think me slow and clumsy. "Jake's asleep. We lost the boat."

He hovered near my elbow, ready to pounce if I slipped again. "Lost the boat? Did you forget to tie it up?"

"Don't I wish." I shook my head slowly as I lowered myself onto the rope seat. When I'd settled, I looked at him straight, ready to gauge his reaction. "Someone shot that boat full of holes and sank it." Let him chew on that. "With Jake and me inside."

Chew he did but not for long. His blue eyes clouded. "You're joking." Confusion fogged the brilliance of his eyes and the precision of his speech. "I mean, you must be."

Genuine surprise or practiced playacting? For the next few minutes, I chewed on those questions while persuading Raphael Tocco of my seriousness. Persuading him, too, of my naïveté as I went into the spiel I'd practiced, hitting hard at buzzwords like *carelessness, coincidence, unintentional*. Nothing sinister, nothing suspicious, just a matter of being at the wrong place at the wrong time. In the end he bought it. Or seemed to.

To be on the safe side, I sat facing him as we raced upriver toward the Boney Creek benchlands, figuring that way I'd get off a shot before he could throw me overboard. No way I wanted another swim in the Yukon. A little conversation might also make that less likely. "I've been reading up on the great migration and find the emerging DNA evidence very impressive."

Raphael Tocco tossed me a smile and raised his eyebrows, inviting further discussion, but his attention remained on the water ahead.

I raised my voice over the whip of the wind and rumble of the engine. "Based on modern natives here and in Siberia, the mitochondrial DNA indicates a common ancestry about forty thousand years ago. Does that date fit your theory?"

Tocco nodded vigorously and shouted a question in return. "Do you trust DNA?"

"Absolutely. If the work's done right." I lifted my shoulders. "Consider the mutation rates and sequence the two DNA. Should work every time."

"Good." His smile reached all the way to his eyes. "A linguist says the native root language separated from Asian origins about thirty-five thousand B.P."

My turn to smile. B.P. is not British Petroleum. B.P. means before present, a new way of measuring time for someone brought up on the B.C. and A.D. model. That's science for you, requiring a separate language for each discipline. How I'd agonized over converting to the metric system and Celsius scale. Measuring by tens does make more sense and

Elizabeth Quinn

should be easier, except for those who've mastered the vast illogic of inches, feet, and yards.

After our arrival at the mouth of Boney Creek, Raphael Tocco restarted the conversation. "I don't think of it as a great migration." He pulled the last knot in the bowline tight and let the rope drop. "In some ways, I don't think Paleolithic peoples even left home."

I hoisted my backpack and headed inland, skirting the boggy patches in the swampy lowlands. "Explain, please."

He came up beside me, matching his stride to mine. "Migration presupposes leaving here and going there. But wouldn't a more natural model be population growth as an ever-widening circle? Think of what happens when you toss a pebble into a still pool."

I scanned the low foothills rising to the south and adjusted our heading to intersect the first site I'd identified with Jake. "I'm listening."

"As man evolved, population increased, requiring a widening of the hunting grounds. Year by year the population increases and mile by mile that population spreads." He threw his arms wide. "And on down through the ages until finally all the world is populated."

Such enthusiasm. At that moment, I found it hard to believe him a mad dog. Instead, I found myself liking him. Again. "To you, this isn't just old bones, is it?"

Raphael Tocco knelt down suddenly and

scooped up a handful of dusty earth. "Look at this." He sifted the soil until a few pale shards surfaced. "Why do you think they call it Boney Creek?"

He plucked the largest fragment and offered it to me. "Animal or human, this once was part of a living creature. Have you ever heard of the Frogman of Veyrier?"

I confessed my ignorance.

"Found near Geneva, along with twelve thousand bones of frogs and toads. A trader or a glutton?" His eyes danced with amusement. "Either way, he is real to me. And then there's Romito the Dwarf."

I snorted. "Late of a Paleolithic straight show?"

He laughed out loud. "Maybe that explains it. He was found in Calabria and, though only four feet tall, lived to be about seventeen. Clearly, he could not have helped much with the hunt, and yet Romito was fed and cared for, perhaps even loved. All those thousands of years ago, so-called primitive humans already possessed the best that is in us. To me, they are real people."

He tilted his hand. The dry earth and bone fragments poured back to the ground. "Probably a lot better people than many of their descendants living today."

For a while, the rising terrain made talking difficult. We walked single file with me leading, and yet I felt no unease with Raphael Tocco at my back. In the light of day and under the sway of his charm, my suspicions seemed groundless, even ludicrous. No wonder Jake liked him. They shared the same wonderful, earnest sweetness. Nothing smarmy or Pollyanna-ish, mind you. What my son and this man had in common was a good heart and an inclination to seek out and prize the best in others. Which is definitely not the stuff from which murderers are made.

In another half hour, we reached the first site, a hot and dusty rise with a steep slope, facing south and with loads of *Artemisia frigida*. Also known as prairie sagewort. I swung off the backpack and pulled out a handful of stakes, a ball of twine, and a measuring tape. Raphael Tocco came up behind me and spun a slow circle on one heel. "Is this it?"

"Yup." I handed him the measuring tape. "The vegetation on this slope is consistent with the pollen samples from Ice Age sediments. We'll mark off a square meter, and then count and catalog everything within it."

Raphael Tocco fed out the metal tape. "Obviously, you want to establish a data base, but why?"

That stopped me. I couldn't hide my surprise. "To preserve it for guys like you." I waved at him to back up and stretch out the tape. "Or don't you think there's anything to be learned from relic vegetation?"

On my signal, he dropped to his knees. "Oh, yes. Absolutely. What we learn just may cause a revolution in the field." He caught the stake I tossed him and worked it into the ground. "The presence of continental glaciers seemed to indicate that the

Beringian steppe had an exceptionally cold and dry environment. Quite unlike what we have here."

"*Artemisia* doesn't like arctic cold." I rolled him the twine, and he tied it on his stake. "But it was the dominant species in the pollen rain from the lake bottom cores. They also found *plantago*—that's plantain—and *chenopodiaceae*—that's goosefoot. Neither are tundra species and both are found here as well."

We worked our way around a square meter, staking and tying our little fence. Our hands and feet and knees bruised the mat of sagewort, releasing a sharp fragrance from the dusty leaves. The woody base of the plant snagged sleeves and socks. When we'd finished setting our limits, Raphael jerked his elbow free and sat back on his heels. "You know they found this plant in the stomach of a mummified mammoth. Perfectly preserved."

"I'm not surprised. Those pollen samples were good, Raphael. A piece of wood dated to thirty-five thousand B.P., and the sediments were undisturbed and unoxidized lake bottom." I studied him across the fenced relic of an ancient time, noting the doubt clouding his blue eyes. "A solution of hydrochloric acid removed any calcium carbonate, and that plus hydrofluoric acid took care of the silica. Cooking and washing with hydrogen peroxide and potassium hydroxide cleansed the sample of organics. What's left was mounted on glycerine jelly and, at six-hundred-power magnification, that ancient pollen looks as fresh as this year's batch."

"Perfectly preserved." He fingered a twig of

Elizabeth Quinn

Artemisia, and his eyes went dreamy. "This is the best we can hope for, I suppose. Dry bones and living plants and mammoth mummies, but not a trace of living man."

He broke off the twig and raised it for closer study. "Without a time machine, I suppose that'll have to do."

19

Only the presence of guests at the Doyon fish camp kept my son from crowing when I returned from my outing unharmed and lacking a suspect in the attack on Delle yet again. Raphael Iocco landed his raft beside two battered sleds and graciously accepted my thanks for twelve hours of backbreaking fieldwork. I'd almost finished my speech when Jake bounded down the path to the beach and, with an expertise derived from years of practice, weighed the sincerity of my thanks and farewell to his friend. As the motor-raft pulled away, heading upstream against the current, his eyes blazed with triumph. "You do like him. A lot."

He sure called that right, but the arrival of another young pup spared me from admitting the truth. At least for a while. Little Adam Demissov charged over the lip of the high bench, surfed a dozen yards on skittering pebbles and plunged headlong into my son's arms. Loss of breath left Jake croaking. "Jesus, kid. Take it easy."

Ever so gently, he set the little boy down on the rocky shore and slowly withdrew hands still poised to steady the wobbling child. "You gotta slow down, man. I'm not kidding."

The little boy raised his flat face and stared at me out of those small, round, wide-set eyes. "Who dat?" He leaned against my son's sturdy leg. "Tsake, who dat?"

Jake laid a reassuring hand on Adam's shoulder. "That's my mom, Adam. You can call her Lauren."

I started to remind him of the afternoon we'd spent picking berries, but Adam wriggled out from under Jake's hand and darted back up the path. I shrugged and tossed my rucksack to Jake. "Obviously one boat is Eleanor's. Who owns the other?"

"We do." Jake slung my pack over one shoulder. "From what Sarah says, it's kind of a spare. Eleanor towed the skiff down from the village." He tossed me a quick glance. "She's planning to stay awhile. To fish."

"Oh, terrific." In the face of my son's smirk, I nodded with great vigor. "I mean it, kiddo. I spent an afternoon with her. She's really not that bad."

That proved to be quite an understatement. Eleanor Demissov turned out to be a lot better than I remembered. Almost jolly, in fact. She allowed Jake to take over with Adam and showed herself to be as handy with a fish knife as Sarah Doyon.

Could be that the traditional rhythms of fish camp soothed her troubled spirit. Or maybe the low murmur of the river stirred her better nature. Whatever the cause, Eleanor actually sang as she worked beside the Grandmother, warbling a song of praise while she moved among the drying racks. She tucked her thick braid up under a ball cap to keep it from swinging into the filleted fish when she bent to hook yet another salmon over the willow pole. When the Grandmother went inside to get dinner, Eleanor kept working. Everything went fine until a glossy black raven swooped into view, circling high overhead and sending Eleanor's mood plummeting back to earth.

I walked up beside her as she squinted against the setting sun to follow the bird's antics. "Jake told me that ravens approach people when the world has gone wrong. Could this be an omen?"

For a few more seconds, she stared at the bird and then reluctantly lowered her eyes to mine. "Perhaps. There has been misfortune. The shooting of Belle Doyon. And the village splintering over oil."

I didn't hide my surprise. "But I thought Raven would be a good omen. After all, Raven is the Creator and so often helps the people."

"What you say is true." Her dark eyes went bleak. "But two nights ago, I heard a raven calling in the darkness. And coming here today, I found a raven floating near the mouth of Boney Creek."

That raised the hair on my neck. "Drowned?"

159

"No." She snorted, apparently disgusted that anyone could suggest such an absurdity. "Not drowned. Shot."

Without any conscious effort, my eyes widened. "Shot! But no one shoots ravens. That's desecration. That's almost like shooting God."

"No one among the *Dene* shoots ravens. None among the *Dene* shoots wolves. And the *Dene* do not shoot each other. But your people do." She looked at me with unblinking eyes. "Your people shoot everything."

That simple observation certainly shut me up. My people do shoot everything. Bulls-eyes, beer cans, road signs, each other—anything and everything is fair game for my people. Don't believe it? Let's do the numbers—33, 575, and 1,116. That's the handgunner's daily toll: 33 women raped, 575 people robbed, and 1,116 others assaulted each and every day in the U.S. of A. On an annual basis, stray bullets killed forty New Yorkers in 1990, handguns kill 22,000 Americans each year, and the United States' domestic weapons pool has reached 200 million firearms. With that kind of firepower, what's another lousy bird, anyway?

I threw the raven another glance and then folded my arms. "Obviously, you think one of my people is responsible. But do you have any idea who specifically did the shooting?"

Eleanor gave me one curt shake and then headed back to the fish-cleaning table. With the last salmon now hung out to dry, all that remained was cleaning up. Jake and Adam took charge of the bones and guts, hauling a brimming plastic bucket down to the river to pitch far out into the current. Eleanor added the day's fish heads, tails, and fins to the cache to be boiled later for the dogs. I rinsed the work table and knives with fresh water, taking care not to slop any gunk onto the dust at my feet. Keeping the drying fish free of flies was tough enough without the attraction of fresh blood. Once we had everything spit-spot, I joined Eleanor at the washing station near the Grandmother's cabin.

I lifted the enamel washbasin off the bent nail pounded into the side of the cabin and set it on a low bench. Eleanor poured in clear, sun-warmed spring water from the five-gallon bucket that Jake filled every morning. I handed her the bar of soap and waited as she lathered up to her elbows. When my turn with the soap came, I returned to the subject at hand. "So you don't know specifically who. How about taking a guess?"

Eleanor occupied herself with sudsing every last bit of fish oil and yuck from her forearms and hands, taking special care with her nails. "Perhaps a man who steals the bones of our dead will also hurt our living."

She dipped a hand into the basin, rinsing her nails free of suds, and then inspected her fingers one by one. "He has been here many weeks this time."

"That may be, but that's still not enough time to turn him into a killer." I cupped handfuls of water over my arms, rinsing away the suds. "I just spent the day with him. He knows I'm suspicious and had plenty of opportunity to do me dirty, but he never made a move."

I stepped away from the wash bench, shook the excess water off my arms, and then grabbed the threadbare towel off another bent nail. "I woke up this morning believing that Raphael Tocco shot Belle, but I'll go to bed tonight knowing he didn't."

I offered Eleanor Demissov the towel. "I'm absolutely convinced that he's innocent."

She took the towel and wiped the water from her arms. "What of the others?" She dried each finger separately. "What of the old one?"

Again she surprised me. "Preston Waite?" A laugh bubbled up my throat. Then I noticed the dead seriousness in Eleanor's eyes. "You're not joking. You really think Dr. Waite shot Belle?"

"Perhaps." She shook out the towel before draping it over the nail. "The raven, the wolf, the *Dene*—all are one to that old man. All are creatures, strangers to his kind. And his kind alone he values."

I looked away, shading my eyes from the glare of the setting sun. Everything she said about the archaeologist was true. He'd hated having Sarah Doyon at his dinner table. He'd barely tolerated Jake's presence. A bigot, yes. But a killer? The man had to be well into his seventies.

Eleanor seemed to sense my internal argument. "Your people make infants of your elders and see them as weak." She spread her hands wide. "But long life truly brings wisdom and strength and endurance. And age doesn't stop wanting. Only with death does wanting end."

"Wanting what?" I turned back to Eleanor, searching her dark eyes for answers I didn't have. "Answer me that. Why would Preston Waite shoot Belle? Why kill wolves or ravens? I'm not sure we'll ever know who until we figure out why."

Instead of an answer, she gave me a shrug and stalked off in the direction of the beach. But the question hung in my mind, echoing my daughter Jessie's words when we first heard about the shooting. "But, Mama, why would anyone want to hurt Belle?" Days later, I still hadn't a clue. I'd questioned a fistful of likely suspects and convinced myself of the innocence of each. Now Eleanor Demissov had pointed to a new suspect, one I found decidedly unlikely. Fortunately, my short and brutal acquaintance with a mousy little murderess named Julianne Blanchard had demonstrated one of the fundamentals of investigation: Never assume the innocence of even the most unlikely person.

High above the fish camp, the solitary raven swooped one final circle before settling on the bough of a spruce tree. I perched on a round of wood near the fire ring. *"Tseek'all,* do you have the answers? Flying high, did you see who and learn why?"

"No question, Mom." Returning from the beach, Jake left the empty pail near Sarah Doyon's worktable before joining me near the fire. "Old Raven sees and knows just about everything. Too bad he squawks instead of talks."

"My turn to squawk, sweetie." I gave Jake my best parrot voice. *"Ggaakk-ggaakk.* You were right about Raphael. *Ggaakk.* You were right."

His wide grin kindled a new light in his eyes, but he managed to stifle an automatic I-told-you-so. Instead, he stated the obvious. "Raphael Tocco is a good guy."

I returned his smile. "You got that right. I wonder how he stands working for that nasty old man."

I tossed in that last bit just to be conversational, but Jake's response took me right back to the problem of who and why. "Nobody sees too much of Dr. Waite. He goes off after breakfast each morning and doesn't come back till just before dinner."

A *zing* of exhilaration coursed through my veins. Talk about energized. If Preston Waite was the latest candidate for who, then his daylong absences from the dig certainly added a new dimension to the question of how. So what if I still didn't know why? That answer would come soon enough. Now that I knew where to look.

20

The endless greens of the Nowitna country made camouflage a snap. From the lowliest moss underfoot to the crowning spruce overhead, the visible world presented variations on a single theme with all things brushed from the same bucket of paint. My gear bag included attire to match—sturdy twill pants in a sun-faded lichen shade, a brushed canvas shirt of jade left dappled by an amateur's washing, and a GI-issue fatigue cap that resisted every attempt to mellow its basic olive drab. The combination might gag a colorist, but Eleanor Demissov admitted that my outfit blended into the background.

"Even I don't see you standing still against the forest." She stayed near the motor in the back of the skiff while I climbed over the side. Her glance flitted over the handgun riding my hip before returning to my face. "I come for you when?"

I dug the heel of my hiking boot into the sand of the narrow beach, still damp with dew though the sun had risen an hour earlier. Jake said Preston Waite returned to the boneyard dig just before dinner. Meaning I'd probably have to miss mine. At least I'd packed enough fruit to see me through.

"Hhhhmmmm." I started to consult my wristwatch but caught myself in time. Outside of the sun, timepieces are irrelevant in the bush. "Let's say an hour before sunset. That'll give me plenty of time to catalog plants."

Her dark eyes narrowed, a response I dismissed as a knee-jerk suspicion of science left over from her antipathy to archaeologists in general and Preston Waite in particular. The night before, I'd described my project on remnant vegetation of the Beringian steppe, explaining my sole purpose as counting, not cutting. She'd asked many questions, including a slew on Raphael Tocco's theories about the land-bridge crossings. But, in the end, Eleanor understood that my "work" would in no way harm her people or their world.

She clenched the handle on the outboard's starter cord. "I return one hour before sunset."

One sharp yank and the motor roared to life again. As the boat backed across the eddy toward the nearest loop of current, Eleanor raised a hand in farewell. A tide of guilt swept through me as I mirrored her gesture. Why hadn't I just told her the truth and asked for her help in tracking Preston Waite?

The skiff wheeled into a tight circle, swinging the bow upstream, as Eleanor smoothly shifted the motor through neutral and into forward gear. Why? The answer to that question came easily. Because I didn't want her superior woods sense showing up my novice skills. In a word—ego. That's why.

I shouldered my day pack and headed into the woods, already chewing on the next question. What if I missed him? The silvery morning light barely penetrated the deep shadows of the forest. What if Preston Waite managed to elude me as I skulked in the bushes? Deep, age-old duff cushioned my steps, muffling the sound of my boots, yet something up ahead heard me and scuttled away. What if I stayed east and the bone doctor went west?

My teeth clenched on edge. Too damn many what-ifs for my taste. Could be that ego of mine would be my undoing. After all, the guy had gotten the drop on a couple of wolves and Belle Doyon. Suddenly that nasty old man loomed rather large, puffed up to true bogeyman proportions. By the time I'd crept in close to the camp near the boneyards, I'd long since fought my ego to a draw. Given another chance, I'd have begged Eleanor Demissov to please, please, please be my leader. Except that nobody but Preston Waite could lead this expedition because he alone knew where we were headed. And why.

I tucked myself into a thicket of birches and waited for the old man to appear. Wildlife biologists get plenty of practice at sitting absolutely still and absolutely quiet for absolutely endless hours of fieldwork. But waiting for Preston Waite was harder, with none of the pleasures of observing animals in a natural setting and entirely too many varieties of unease clawing at my innards. Every flying insect that buzzed past my ear and every crawling insect that crept over my hand engendered a shudder that needed suffocating immediately. My fear that I'd miss him battled my fear that I wouldn't until blessedly? . . . cursedly? . . . finally, the old man strode into view.

Preston Waite came within two yards of my hiding spot, carrying a sturdy walking stick topped by an elaborate carving, and humming a cheerful tune that sounded to my untrained ears like something by Mozart. As he passed by, leading with his chin, I noted the canvas pack strapped to his shoulders but saw no sign of a gun, .25-caliber or otherwise. With his nose stuck up so high, he probably never found an artifact from the Paleolithic unless he tripped over it. Which boded well for my surveillance. By the looks of him, being followed was the last thing on his mind.

I gave the old man a count of fifty and then another. A glance at my watch showed that nearly two minutes had passed. Time enough? Probably.

Sluggish, blood-starved muscles slowed me a bit, forcing me to do a couple of deep stretches before I could start after him. That launched another balloon of fear that I'd lose him before I even got started. His passage left sign the greenest *cheechako* could read—clumps of crushed grass, scuffed mats of needles, clear boot prints in a few dusty spots. Still, I considered quickening my steps to a jog. The brightening ahead meant he'd be leaving the forest's shelter. In more open country, I'd have to keep way back, far enough to lose him among the gentle hills and valleys contouring the land. And yet some instinct actually slowed my steps to a tortoise's creep. I edged forward to discover him standing among the last fringe of trees in the woods, stiff with concentration as he scanned the country ahead through a pair of high-powered binoculars.

Again I hid, but Preston Waite never looked back. Talk about confidence! The old man had no doubt his word was law to his underlings. No one would follow. No one would dare. As a parent, I knew that kind of authority had only one source: terror. And that knowledge freed me from fear. Lord Acton got it right: Absolute power corrupts absolutely. The bigoted old bully that I followed thought himself a giant surrounded by soft-headed cowards. And that delusion would bring him down. Another fundamental of investigation: Always look back.

And so when Preston Waite left the taiga, the great boreal forest that swaths the northern reaches of the continent, I tagged along behind. On another day, crossing the flatlands would have been a joy because a carpet of wildflowers nodded in the light breeze—bluebells, irises, monkshood, fireweed, and wild roses in the dry stretches, with yellow and dwarf pond lilies dominating the wetlands. The old man flushed a pair of trumpeter swans, which rose from the water, wings gently beating as they cooed *woo-ho, woo-woo, woo-ho.* On another day I might have lingered to admire that spectacular tableaux, but way out in front, Preston Waite's silhouette began to shrink. First his feet vanished. Then his legs. And his torso. Until at last even his upturned chin sank from sight below the next ridgeline.

I kicked into higher gear, jouncing along at a slow trot, aiming for the spot where the crown of his straw hat had slipped from view. His heading now pointed east, toward Boney Creek and the benchlands with their weird topography. The place in some ways resembled a miniature Monument Valley, with a series of sandy mesas carved by small creeks. Melting Ice Age glaciers probably deposited the layers of sand way back when. In the centuries since, each spring runoff carved the channel deeper, exposing yet another cache of the fossils from which the locale took its name. A bone doctor's idea of heaven, you'd think, and the one up ahead definitely wanted the place all to himself. Which again raised the inevitable question—Why?

I crested the ridge in the shade cast by a patch of poplar and spotted Preston Waite below, his yellow straw hat a beacon amid all that green. My lookout afforded a panorama of the benchlands. Maybe I should take advantage of the view to see where he went? My gut told me that his destination lay somewhere in that maze of mesas. But lately my gut was wrong more often than it was right. And staying there risked losing the old man entirely if his path merely cut across Boney Creek before disappearing into the woods beyond.

Preston Waite decided the issue by choosing that moment to stop once again to survey the area ahead through his binoculars. I hunkered down in the shade and pulled out my own pair of spyglasses. He scanned the landscape in a 180-degree arc, coming back time and again to an area about a half-mile ahead of him and slightly north. A spring-swollen creek had undercut the side of one mesa, undermining the roots of trees that now hung horizontal above summer-dry creek bed. Probably carved a cave, too, though the gloom cast by the sweeper trees masked any opening. I did discern the vague outline of something else in the deep shade. Actually three somethings that appeared to hang below the tilted trees. Probably just broken branches.

I turned my attention back to the old man just in time. He pulled the binoculars from around his neck and swung the pack from his back. In went the binocs and out came . . . a gun? My heart ripped into a high gear. A gun. A small, dark gun that lay across his palm for a moment while he checked it out. Awkwardly. Gingerly. Like a man forced to touch something odious. And then Preston Waite started forward, heading toward the cut bank, leading with a stiff upraised arm that pointed the way with the small gun clenched in its fist. Awkward, amateurish, but accurate if indeed he'd aimed that gun at Belle Doyon and the two wolves that had turned up on the Grandmother's doorstep. All of which urged caution, and so I elected to remain in the shade atop the ridge and merely watch. At least for a while.

That while stretched into hours. Preston Waite beelined to that cut bank and disappeared into the gloom. As the minutes crept past, I stayed in place, eyes glued to my binoculars, shifting position as comfort and the sun's angle demanded. My protection of shade shortened to virtually nothing at noon, forcing me to seek refuge in the leafy recesses of the poplar, where I peeled and ate two bananas. Still, the gloom remained beneath the horizontal trees atop the cut bank.

Eventually, the westering sun cast new shade, allowing me to climb out of the trees. Another orange, another hour, still no sign of the bone doctor. The only real news was that the lowering sun and shifting shadows had lightened the gloom under the horizontal trees. Definitely something hanging there, three long rectangular shapes. And then, as the light shifted, the first of those shapes grew paws. The gloom shifted, and the second grew paws. By that time, the first had legs.

Slowly, slowly, the minutes crept past and the light crept under those hanging trees. Just as slowly, my stomach grew queasy from anticipation and horror. By the time the third shape had grown his paws, the second had legs and the first had a snout. A toothy, grinning snout. Very wolfish. And very dead.

I let the binoculars drop into my lap. For some sick and unimaginable reason, Preston Waite had strung up three dead wolves in a macabre festoon for his cave of shadows. Why? I didn't know. And in that moment, I didn't want to know. Not when. Not why. Not anything.

21

Preston Waite hadn't skinned his festoon of wolves. From ten yards out, the stench almost gagged me. I searched the Vicks Vap-o-Rub out of my pack and smeared enough in each nostril to mask the reek of rotting flesh. And then I crossed the last stretch of dry creek bed and ducked under the overhanging branches.

An hour earlier, the old man had emerged from the farthest gloom of the cut bank and made ready to leave. As he fussed with his gun and binoculars and pack, I withdrew to a thicket of willows, sheltering deep inside the buzzing, bug-ridden brush and straining to see through the dense shrubbery. He finally plodded by, chin still held high but step decidedly slower, so I gave him a fifteen-minute start before crawling out of my hidey-hole. Then I swung off in a wide arc, reconnoitering toward the river as I moved ever closer to the stinking mess beneath the sweeper trees. Once or twice, a prickle of skin suggested I wasn't alone, but each time a careful spyglass survey proved my gut wrong again. A full forty-five minutes passed before I arrived within smelling distance of Preston Waite's secret.

I could not help looking at those suppurating carcasses, each strung up by the tail and crawling with arthropods. Which made my own skin crawl. Scientist or not, I've never claimed to be unmoved by the violence and ugliness of nature's recycling mode. But distancing allows the fascination to emerge, and with conscious effort I switched into science gear by formulating a question: How long had the wolves been dead?

That proved to be a very tough call. The animals had moved into and out of the stiffening known as rigor mortis, suggesting many days had passed. And several things reinforced that impression: bones exposed by shrinking skin; hollow, picked-clean eye sockets; entrails protruding from burst bellies. Yet, overall the carcasses retained an amazing structural integrity. The overarching trees produced a sheltering roof that protected from both the heat of the sun and the battering of the rain. The drop in temperature when I ducked under the trees had pushed up gooseflesh on my arms. That cool air surely slowed decomposition. Then again, wasn't the temperature a lot colder than even the deepest shade produced?

All that time, my eyes had been adjusting from the brightness of the sunlit creek bed to the shadows of the cut-bank cavern. Just when I could see better, I wanted to see more, wanted to step deeper into the gloom. And with each step I took, the air chilled noticeably, dramatically, until true shivers overtook me. I swung my pack to the ground and crouched over it, hands shaking as I drew a Polartec pullover from the bottom pocket. And then I spotted the cave.

Beneath the tangle of undermined roots, the creek had sculpted a shallow cavern. And within that sandy cavern, the swollen waters had unearthed a tumble of huge boulders that formed a cave. Above the cave, the cavern wall showed the telltale glisten of an ice wedge, one of the buried sheets of ice that are a peculiar feature of permafrost. From the cave came a narrow trickle of water, indicating more ice within. I dug the small flashlight out of my pack, tested the light and, when it shone, headed for the cave.

My circle of light lit the water dripping over the cave's rocky threshold. Rock below, too. Maybe bedrock? My beam moved inside, highlighting the edge of a wall of milky ice. I knelt on the threshold of the cave, panning my light up to find the ceiling just inches above my head. And then I aimed my beam lower, panning along the wall of ice and across patches of darker ice. Until I recognized the shape locked in one dark patch of ice.

A hand.

I flinched back, smacking my head against rock and clattering my flashlight against the wall of ice.

A human hand.

My stomach knotted. The beam of my flashlight spread over the wall of ice, highlighting the dark patches that arranged themselves into a silhouette of a man crouched mere inches within the ice. As I crouched mere inches without. Jesus! Preston Waite had to be some kind of sicko. Killing wolves and stringing them up. Killing a man and icing him down. The utter absurdity of my last thought caught me just as the beam of my light caught the neat row of points laid out beside the frozen man. Unquestionably knapped flint. Meaning very, very, very old. The Ice Man, too?

Framing that question restored my equilibrium. Dr. Maxwell replaced Lauren the Horrified. Whatever catastrophe befell the frozen man was the work of nature, not Preston Waite. Even through the thin shroud of ice, I could see that the Ice Man's body was brown and dried out, resembling the mummified carcasses of mammoths and bison sometimes discovered at placer mines in the Fairbanks area. The oldest of those finds dated as far back as 35,000 B.P., long before the crossing of the land bridge. Discovering a man anywhere near that old would definitely be the find of a lifetime. Probably the biggest find of the century. Possibly the greatest find in the history of archaeology. And maybe even a find worth killing for.

An image of Belle Doyon flashed through my

mind, her body motionless and swathed in white, trapped in her way just as the Ice Man had been trapped. By being in the wrong place at the wrong time. Somehow she'd happened upon Preston Waite or his once-in-a-lifetime find, probably without even realizing the significance. Which was why she never connected the wolf pelts that turned up on the Grandmother's doorstep with whatever— old man or cold cave—she stumbled across near Boney Creek. Exactly what message those pelts were supposed to deliver was beyond reach of my most astute reasoning.

Overcoming my incipient claustrophobia, I crawled deeper into the cave, closer to that neat row of points. One short of a dozen. As I bent closer to see without touching, my light glinted off a stray edge in the wall of ice. The edge of a hole. A very symmetrical round hole. A drill hole.

I laid my cheek against the cold, wet rock floor of the cave and sighted one eye down the short length of that hole to discover one finger of the Ice Man's other hand. The skin appeared shriveled but intact, including the nail, yet somehow curiously flattened at the tip.

Raising my head an inch above the stone floor of the cave, I blinked my eyes a few times and then, lowering back into position, I refocused on the interior end of that tiny tunnel. Make that finger mostly intact. The tip had been clipped with surgical precision, halfway down the nail. A sample?

I fingered the tips of my own digits, finding the bone quite close to the surface. A sample, all right, and one that included bone. Most likely for the collagen, the material that works best for radiocarbon dating. Which explained why the old man hadn't already announced his find to the world. He wanted to be damn sure of his facts before claiming the crowning achievement of his remarkable scientific career. That insight suggested a new, complicating factor to what had started out as a simple case of right and wrong: science. All of a sudden, what was good for Belle also had to be good for science.

I lifted myself from the floor of the cave and wiggled around until my back rested against one boulder and the toes of my boots against another. The beam of my flashlight flickered once before steadying into a dimmer circle of light. With the little time remaining, I systematically covered that wall of ice, noting the many seeping drain holes Preston Waite had drilled. One led to something fashioned of fur that also showed signs of clipping. Probably part of the Ice Man's clothing. Most of the others dotted the ice wall in a random pattern, perhaps clustered a bit toward the bottom to assist gravity in draining the cave of its prison of ice.

My arm grew tired from holding the flashlight as I moved it slowly over the ice wall, imaginary grid by imaginary grid. A line of shallow depressions in the ice near the floor suggested the source of the knapped flint points lined up so neatly by Dr. Waite. Perhaps the Ice Man sheltered in the cave during a storm, spending the hours flaking flint points for his weapons until finally overcome by hunger or cold. Some work ethic. Maybe the Ice Man was the first true WASP in America.

I panned the light over the stone floor of the cave, finding no evidence of a fire. But that, too, could be locked in the ice awaiting discovery. Again the light flickered and then steadied into a dimmer halo. Soon the batteries would be drained, and I had a ways to go through dark woods before meeting Eleanor back at the river. I thumbed off the flashlight and scrambled toward the threshold of the cave.

Outside under the sweeper trees, the festoon of wolves swayed in the evening breeze, grisly sentinels guarding an ancient secret. Against what? Did Preston Waite honestly believe a couple of rotting wolves would protect his Ice Man from roaming predators? But while rotting meat usually attracted predators, this grim trio showed no sign of feeding. Indicating that he'd tainted the meat somehow and thereby tainted the place as well. Very clever, very slick, and another reminder that the old man must not be underestimated.

I ducked under the low-slung branches, pausing on the dry creek bed to orient myself and wipe the Vicks from my nostrils. No lights beyond the night's first stars showed against the growing darkness. No need to worry about Preston Waite right now. He'd long since arrived at his camp. And until the slow drip of melting ice freed the frozen secret in the cave, that old man was going nowhere. Meaning I had time to think, time to plan, and time to perfect the details of whatever came next.

After refreshing myself with a deep breath of warm but clean air, I set off, angling toward the ridge where I'd hidden from Preston Waite. The skin of my neck prickled, a primitive alarm that I ignored. Lately, my instincts had been wrong too often. At that moment, I actually doubted that my gut would ever be right again.

22

My discovery of the Ice Man left me with a real predicament: how to achieve justice for Belle and safeguard a momentous advance for science. Only the truly naive still believe that scientists inexorably seek truth. Consider the researcher who "proves" his hypothesis by faking the results of his study, or the Ph.D. who fashions his expert testimony to fit the "facts" of the legal team paying his fee. Every scientific advance breaks as many careers as it makes, and the Ice Man was no exception. For Preston Waite's theory to rise, the theory of somebody else had to fall, a powerful incentive for sabotaging truth. And personal baggage like an attempted murder charge would make such sabotage ridiculously easy.

Long after everyone else at the Doyon fish camp had found sleep, I lay awake in the loft, fussing my down sleeping bag into knots as I grappled with my dilemma. Just hours earlier, on my way to meet Eleanor, I'd made a couple of preliminary decisions, including one to let her in on the secret and enlist her help in keeping Preston Waite under surveillance. But at the boat, her sullen greeting and glowering eyes forced me to rethink that plan. What made me imagine a radical native with a grudge against white archaeologists would help me safeguard an "artifact" like the Ice Man? The Vicks I'd stuffed up my nose must have pickled my brain. Clearly, I couldn't depend on Eleanor Demissov.

As the short, subarctic night closed down around us, I considered other candidates for the job, focusing first on my son. Jake and Adam danced around the leaping flames of the campfire, a Mutt and Jeff pair of spinning tops matched only in their enthusiasm for fire and fun. Their laughter rose into the air like an eruption of glowing sparks, with Jake's lower register providing a bass line to Adam's higher-pitched trilling. For days I'd seen the man my son would soon become. That night I saw the child who had not yet been outgrown. Jake's grace under the pressure of a sniper's attack had reaffirmed his self-esteem. No way I'd test his courage or risk his life again any time soon.

After the fire dwindled to embers and I climbed the ladder to the loft, Sarah Doyon also had been eliminated from my list of potential allies. That left only one candidate: Raphael Tocco. No matter how much I liked the boy wonder with the great haircut, could I trust him when my target was the mentor he revered? Add to that question the Ice Man wrinkle. Whether two thousand years old or twenty thousand years old, that frozen mummy represented the fulfillment of Raphael Tocco's dreams and wishes and hopes and prayers. After years of digging dusty holes and sifting broken bones, he longed to discover something whole and human. So he hadn't killed me the day we counted the Beringian remnants on the hills above Boney Creek. That didn't mean he'd help me bring down his professional idol. Especially when collaring Preston Waite risked tainting the discovery he so fervently desired. Like a fledgling poised on the brink of flight, Raphael Tocco would need the shelter of the old man's professional standing to introduce such a revolutionary find to the archaeological world. That conclusion crossed the last candidate off my list, leaving me on my own.

Somewhere off in the distance, an owl hooted and, more from habit than from interest, I started counting.

Hoo, hoo-hoo-hoo, hoo-oo, hoo-oo.

Eight hoots meant a female of the taxonomic classification *Bubo virginianus* or, more commonly, the great horned owl, also known as the cat owl. The first time I'd heard one in the wild, I was sleeping under the stars with Max in a lonely little valley high in California's Sierra Nevada mountains. Conditioned by a slew of bad movies, I stiffened, much to Max's amusement. He answered back as a male, with a rhythm of five hoots. The owl hooted again and again, moving closer all the time, until finally she sailed out of the night on silent wings, swooping just out of reach before vanishing into the darkness. For many years, the hooting of a solitary owl had heartened me, but the owl at the Doyon fish camp hollowed me out, reminding me of how much I'd lost before filling me with longing for Max. For the scent of him. For the warmth of him. For the strength of him. I never wanted to go it alone. Now I had no choice.

I unwadded the sleeping bag around my hips, trying to find a position comfortable enough to induce sleep. Nothing had to be decided that night. Preston Waite wasn't going anywhere without his discovery, and the Ice Man remained in the deep freeze. Still, caution demanded that I watch the old man closely, even if that meant rising every morning before dawn to spend my days crouched in a thicket overlooking the Boney Creek benchlands. Which would, on a more positive note, provide plenty of space and solitude for figuring out how to bring the discoverer to justice and his discovery safely to light. In the morning, I'd ask Eleanor for a ride across the river again. She'd do that much for me, at least.

Yawning, I snuggled deeper into my sleeping bag. Some practical matters also needed attention. Like preserving the body once the ice melted . . . and preventing contamination . . . and transportation . . . and . . .

Much later I awoke to find the sun high and Eleanor long gone. The Grandmother had taken young Adam on another berry-picking expedition, leaving me snoring in the loft and my son whittling beforc the cold ashes of the campfire. As I breakfasted al fresco on stale pilot bread and lukewarm tea, Jake quickly detected my annoyance at finding my plans thwarted yet again.

"No sweat, Mom. I'll take you anywhere you want to go."

The casual words didn't belie his downcast posture, the slumping shoulders that told me my preference for Eleanor's taxi service hurt. Which was great. Just great. Now I had Jake's self-esteem to worry about. Again. On top of everything else. No wonder our heroic archetypes are usually loners. A hero with a family wouldn't get anything done. Except raising that family. And come to think of it, more and more that's a job that requires a heroic helping of courage.

"Thanks for the offer, sweetie." Across the dead campfire, he stiffened, hearing the "but" even before I spoke the word. Still, I couldn't put him at risk again. No way. Not again. "But won't the Grandmother need you here?"

"Nah." The blade of his knife struck deeply at the stick in his hand. "I already emptied the box trap on the fish wheel. And she trusts me with her boat."

Trapped! Boxed in like a salmon after a ride on Yukon River fish wheel. Though my fate didn't include execution, I felt as desperate as those fish that flailed against the walls of the trap, beating themselves bloody. Aaarrggghhh! No escape. Not unless I gave up the idea of stalking Preston Waite.

And damn me as a rotten mother, I simply couldn't do that.

"Sounds good." Everything but my voice, which actually sounded way too bright. And soooo phoney. I modulated a bit. "I'll just pack some snacks. You can hang out with Raphael or come back for me later. Whatever."

"Couldn't I come with you?" He carefully wiped the knife blade across his jeans, so carefully that his eyes never strayed in my direction. "I could carry your pack and help you count those stupid plants. Whatever."

While my "whatever" promised freedom, Jake's "whatever" positively groveled, sniveling and downtrodden, just enough to open a crack in that servile facade. Factor in his use of the word *stupid*. In the context of stupid plants, the word connotes anger. All of which added up to manipulation, and that hardened my heart. For reasons I didn't take time to fathom, Jake had decided to arouse my guilt and run a dodge. One I no longer bought.

"Sorry, kiddo, I gotta cover a lot of ground and you'd just slow me down."

That got his attention. He raised his head, eyes snapping. "What a bunch of bull. I can outhike you standing still."

Jake took special pride in his endurance, a vanity I often challenged to bend him to my will. But the only challenge that interested me that day was Preston Waite. "Maybe so, but I can't spare time to find out."

"But, Mom, I'm tired of digging. It's so boring

and I get so hot." He paused, searching my face for a reaction, before continuing with his new tactic. "And I can't stay here. That brat Adam won't get outta my face."

Downshifting into a whine sealed Jake's fate. He reverted to classic kid so I reverted to classic mom. I'd already rescued my son's self-esteem. Before I'd put him at risk again, I'd wring his darling little neck.

"Then bring a book and spend the day reading." I absolutely gushed. "School starts in a couple of weeks and you still haven't finished your reading list."

The expression on Jake's face suggested that I'd totally wigged out. I suppose I did resemble a standard issue mother from the black and white days of 1950s sitcom TV. Except for the .45-caliber Colt automatic riding my hip. That was nineties all the way.

23

Jake decided the last of his summer reading—George Orwell's *Animal Farm*—could wait for another day. When we got to the archaeological site at the boneyards, he asked Raphael Tocco to put him to work and landed the tedious job of sifting buckets of earth through a framed screen to rescue any overlooked chips of bone or flint. Much to my surprise, my son didn't complain. He didn't even shoot me a dirty look as he headed toward his workstation across the dig site. I stayed just long enough to make sure Preston Waite had stuck to his usual schedule. A casual inquiry wouldn't seem amiss.

"I don't see Dr. Waite anywhere." For effect, I faked a nice little frown to match the earnest look I leveled on Raphael. "I hope he's not sick."

"A little annoyed, perhaps, but not sick in the

least." At my raised eyebrows, he continued. "He's the featured speaker at an important symposium next month and hasn't even started writing his monograph. I suggested he spend an hour at his desk this morning. Actually, I insisted." The young scientist shrugged. "He just hates getting started."

"I know exactly how he feels." My feigned sympathy included a deep sigh as I checked my watch. "Poor old guy. Don't you think he's done enough for one day? You should let him come out and play."

Raphael Tocco loosed a chime of laughter. "He's come out and gone out. Walking that is. That's how he spends his days—taking long, solitary walks. He says the walking helps him think. And in that solitude, he writes the monograph—in his head."

I widened my eyes, looking suitably amazed at such genius. "Wish I could work that way."

I tilted my face to the sun and spread my arms to embrace the entire glorious summer day. "Even something as simple as counting plants comes hard for me on a day like this."

After a few seconds, I lowered my face and gave Raphael Tocco a final smile. "Still, I better get started. Unless I want to be counting plants when the snow flies."

I followed the trail that led to the archaeologist's camp and then reconnoitered until I located a path that seemed the obvious choice for anyone heading to the benchlands. Meaning the trail angled in the right direction. The only bit of information I hadn't gotten was the approximate time of Preston Waite's departure. Still, that was no cause for panic. I already knew his destination. And by keeping a sharp eye ahead I'd make sure not to overtake him. After the excitement of yesterday, I'd enjoy a more sedate walk in the woods. And knowing in detail what lay within the shadows cast by the sweeper trees meant I could kick back a bit at my lookout on the ridge. As long as the Ice Man remained safely frozen in his cave, I had plenty of time to make my plans.

Stray shafts of light penetrated the thick canopy of branches overhead and, though no breeze stirred, last season's fall of needles perfumed the forest air with the rich tang of spruce. I ambled along at a steady pace, savoring the scent as I studied the trail for sign. Here and there, a mound of scat marked an intersection with an animal trail. Grizzlies preferred more open country but plenty of other critters liked the woods. Eventually, I came across my own sign—the imprint of my boot sole, complete with manufacturer's logo. I knew a moment's unease, wondering if Preston Waite had noticed my track. Then I remembered the old man's posture, leading with his upthrust chin, and marveled again at his ability to spot fossils.

At the fringe of the woods I paused long enough to scope out the country ahead through my binoculars. No one in sight. That finding held true for the next mile or so. At the top of every rise I raised the binoculars and scanned ahead. My surveys revealed no sign of Preston Waite, but that didn't alarm me. No uncertainty about his destination, after all. And I had ice as old as time on my side.

Then all at once I spotted him. Or thought I did. From my vantage point on the last rise before the ridge that marked the start of the Boney Creek benchlands, I spied a patch of color ahead. Yellow. And moving.

I let the binoculars drop and laughed out loud. Again the old man's straw hat was my beacon. And at almost the same spot! When I looked again, the scrap of yellow had vanished, just as I'd expected. He'd begun his descent of the ridge.

Talk about ego! Mine started to inflate at a rate that matched the expansion of the universe in the moments after the big bang. Did I have great woods sense or what? Finding my own sign on the trail! Not to mention people sense—the old man matched my expectations every step of the way! Before I had a chance to get really carried away with my own brilliance, Dr. Preston Waite delivered a pinprick that instantly deflated my burgeoning ego.

He roared.

That howl pinned me in place, locking my feet and leaving me breathless. Such rage! Such fury! If murder could speak, Preston Waite's bellow might be its voice. Even safely out of reach and out of sight, his wordless shriek left me cowering. No one could doubt the age-old meaning of that yowl: blood lust.

Then the old man punctuated his rage in the

modern way. *BANG-BANG-BANG*. Instantly, my mind compared the puny whine of his .25 with the full-throated bark of my .45. Which reminded me of the gun I wore. Which persuaded me to get moving. No matter what caused the old man's outburst, I carried the stopper on my hip.

I tore off at a dead run. Probably a grizzly. Plenty of spawning salmon in Boney Creek.

The toe of my boot caught a nub of rock, launching me sideways. I threw out an arm to regain my balance. But ripe flesh beats fresh fish. And wolves don't scare bears. Not three wolves. Not dead wolves. And, apparently, not even tainted wolves.

Thorny bushes clutched at my twill pants, but I tore loose without slowing. The griz probably caught a whiff of the Ice Man from those drill holes. And put those long, sharp claws to good use. *BANG-BANG-BANG*.

The day pack whumped against my back and shoulders, but who had time to cinch it down? Good thing I'd tied my holster. I'd need the .45. That second volley of shots confirmed my theory. Had to be a grizzly. Lesser beasts would have skedaddled after the first round. Had to be a griz. Just my luck to own the stopper. The old man's .25 certainly couldn't. If he had time to reload.

I flew over the lip of the ridge above Boney Creek, trusting my trajectory to the memory of a gradual slope. My feet skidded a ways before catching. Then my landing steadied, giving me a chance to see instead of speculate.

My headlong dash had shaved many yards from the old man's lead. He'd made it to the bottom of the ridge and started across the benchlands, angling toward the site of his miraculous find. But even with the slower pace his age required, I might have trouble catching up. And any grizzly can outrun the fastest human. Maybe I could stop the old man in time.

I skidded to a stop, intending to warn him off with a bellow of my own. That's when I finally looked far enough ahead to discover the true cause of Preston Waite's frenzy. I didn't need my binoculars to see the changes wrought in a single night: the wolves removed from their gallows, the trees stripped of their branches, the Ice Man freed from his frozen grave.

My breath caught in my throat. A pile of spruce branches rose above the dry creek bed in a mound surrounded by the suppurating carcasses of the wolves, topped by the Ice Man in his frozen crouch and guarded by a dark-haired woman with a single braid. Eleanor Demissov.

Down below and now way too far ahead, Preston Waite also stopped running. Sunlight glinted off the barrel of the .25-caliber as he thumbed in bullets. Then he started off again, angling toward the place where Eleanor waited, his trot a little faster.

Fear clamped around me like a vise, momentarily strangling my cry of warning. After all those hours of practice, I had a living target. But not the bear I'd counted on.

As I reached down to release the safety strap on my holster, I let loose the biggest shout I could manage. Then another. And another. Each tinged with despair. All those hours of practice inexorably led to this target. A living man. But first, I had to catch him.

24

My living target had a living target of his own, and she proved tough to catch. Not that Eleanor Demissov gave up her ground, although that's exactly what I feared as I dashed down the ridge and across the braided streams, zigzagging around the mesas that formed the Boney Creek benchlands. The only thing I heard above my own ragged breathing was the bark of Preston Waite's .25-caliber pistol. Talk about terror! Jesus.

By the time I reached the pile of spruce branches, he'd wounded her and run her to ground at one end of the mound. She lay on her back on the rocky creek bed, spitting defiance as blood seeped from one arm, scrabbling with her legs and good arm to escape, making inches when she needed miles. Preston Waite followed her inch by inch, taunting her in a hoarse and breathless voice, brandishing the gun that cut down Belle Doyon.

"That's enough, Waite." Ten yards out from my living target, I sighted in on the middle of his back and suddenly needed all my concentration to keep from pulling the trigger. "Your .25 draws blood, but my .45 leaves big holes. Put down the popgun."

That shut him up and shut him down. Except for his heaving chest, the old man didn't move; even his gun arm froze in place. Eleanor kept scrabbling, making feet and then yards as I moved forward, maintaining my shooting stance. When she finally scuttled around the branch pile and out of sight, I stood just three feet behind Preston Waite.

"Drop the popgun or I'll drop you." The words came out a growl. "If you have any doubts, old man, then think about this. Belle Doyon is a very good friend. And I owe her."

He signaled his submission with a shrug and slowly lowered the hand holding the gun, following my order to toss it clear. Then just as slowly, he turned to face me, arms spread wide. "Dr. Maxwell, I'm sure you understand the importance of my find."

I held my position, gun now leveled on the middle of his chest. He didn't seem eager to test me and never even glanced at the pistol he'd tossed aside.

"You are a scientist." His frantic gesture toward the Ice Man atop the mound of spruce belied his calm words. "Surely you understand the barbarity of removing my find from the cave. And I know you will prevent the atrocity that creature has planned."

A smirk pursed my lips. "What's your definition of atrocity, Dr. Waite?"

"Cremation." He shuddered and closed his eyes. "That creature intends to incinerate my find."

That shut me up. I risked a glance at the mound of branches. Of course. Eleanor had built a funeral pyre for the Ice Man, a cultural artifact the archaeologist recognized on sight. No wonder he'd been frantic. At the same time, I'd been so frantic to rescue Eleanor I never gave a thought to what she'd been doing. Or why.

"You won't let that creature burn my find, will you?" He took a step toward me. "Tell me you'll stop this atrocity!"

His word choice pissed me off. "That creature" for Eleanor and "my find" for the Ice Man. Plus he'd managed to distract me from an injured woman, which only added to my anger.

I flicked my gun in the direction I wanted him to take. "I'm not telling you anything until I see Eleanor. Now move it."

Eleanor hadn't gone far. And she hadn't changed her plans for the Ice Man. We found her crouched on the other side of the bonfire, struggling to strike a spark with her good arm. She'd emptied her fire bag on the ground before her—tinder, shavings, and drill cord—and held her flint in one hand and the pyrite in the other. Although the hand of her wounded arm proved too weak to grasp either flint

198

or pyrite securely enough to strike a spark, she kept trying.

I came up beside her and swung the pack off my back, moving awkwardly because of the gun in my hand. "I've got a first aid kit in here. Let's take care of that arm."

She didn't bother to look up or give up her attempt to strike a spark. "And let the old one steal away with my ancestor?"

She had a point. From the sounds of his pleas, Preston Waite hadn't given up either. And he definitely hadn't gotten it. Somehow, despite the gun I had leveled on him, he thought we were on the same side. Maybe in terms of science. But in no other way. In the face of his far less than abject defeat, I didn't dare turn my back on him. Not before I'd tied him down, anyway.

I nudged my pack toward Eleanor. "Unlace the waist strap, will you?"

After wrapping a figure eight around his wrists and cinching the strap tight, I led Preston Waite to a shady spot, sat him down in front of a good-size rock, and tied the rest of the strap around the rock. First he reasoned, then he begged, and finally he cursed, but I would not be moved. His vilest invective turned out to be as quaint as his notion of right and wrong. Only when I turned away from him to concentrate on Eleanor's wound did he fall silent.

Eleanor flinched when I helped her out of the plaid sweater and paled considerably when I pulled the blood-soaked cloth away from her wound.

Preston Waite's bullet had plowed a short furrow across her arm a few inches below the shoulder. I injected more confidence into my voice than I actually felt. "Doesn't look too bad."

After dipping a cotton ball in fresh water from my bottle, I blotted the wound as long as either of us could stand, which couldn't have been even a minute. Then I smeared the jagged flesh with the antibiotic ointment my family calls miracle goop, covered the mess with a sterile pad, and oh-so-gently secured the bandage with about a yard of gauze. Throughout my ministrations Eleanor's eyes had teared, but she hadn't sobbed or moaned. And when at last I flourished a sling to support her wounded arm, she actually smiled. "Thank you, Lauren. For everything."

"Don't thank her yet." Preston Waite tugged against the rock that held him down, grunting with effort. "She won't let you destroy my find. No scientist would dare. Go ahead, ask her. Ask her!"

Eleanor didn't speak, only watched with calm and patient eyes as I fastened the sling around her neck. Our silence drove Preston Waite into a frenzy. "Answer me, damn you! Will you protect my find? I demand that you answer me this minute! Tell me you will protect my find from this creature! Now, I say!"

I gave Eleanor's good arm a squeeze and then sat back on my heels, ready to deal with her attacker. Also Belle's attacker. Fury purpled his face and a snarl twisted his lips. He jerked against the strap that bound him, succeeding in moving the rock, but not very far. In the end, drained of energy by rage and impotence, he slumped forward, resting his head against the rock that held him. "Dr. Maxwell, I implore you. Please say you'll preserve my find."

The magic word! Having finally heard it, I had to respond. Especially since my opponent had exhausted himself and was too weak to fight back. "Tell me about your find. What's the date on him?"

He hesitated only an instant. "At least twenty-two thousand B.P. and perhaps a good deal older. The collagen sample wasn't quite enough."

Maybe not, but I still got quite a hit off the Ice Man's age. The excitement that zinged through my veins left me light-headed. Older than Nebuchadnezzar and the hanging gardens he built in Babylon! Older than King Tut and all the pyramids in Egypt! Older than just about everything on earth, except for flakes of rock and broken bones. And the Ice Man was whole. Not a twenty-two-thousand-year-old fragment but a whole, entire man! I'd suspected as much, but still the truth left me dazzled.

Preston Waite sensed exactly that and pressed his point. "We have not a moment to lose, Dr. Maxwell. After spending those eons encased in ice, my find cannot withstand thawing. Even as we dither, the sun is destroying my discovery."

The warning hit hard and I scrambled to my feet, eager to rescue the Ice Man. But Eleanor Demissov grabbed one of my hands and stopped me. " 'My find,' the old one says, but he was a man. And he is ancestor to the *Dene.*"

As gently as possible, I freed my hand and took a step back. "We don't have to make any final decisions right now. The Ice Man probably is an ancestor of your people. But he's an incredibly important discovery for all people."

She started to protest, but I wouldn't listen. "Just stop, okay? I'm not going to decide one way or the other. That's definitely not my decision to make."

I backed off another step and shot a glance at Preston Waite, who looked eager, hopeful. "What I'm going to do is climb up there and see what kind of shape he's in. And that's all I'm going to do."

I scrambled up the pile of spruce branches, needing elbows, hands, knees, and feet to reach the top, where I balanced precariously next to the Ice Man. Eyes as brown as his skin stared up at me, sunken into sockets but definitely whole. A thin layer of flesh covered the flat bones of his cheeks, so like Belle's. And Eleanor's. The garment he wore hung in shreds, tattered beyond identification though I knew his clothing must have been made of fur and hide. And showing through the torn hide were patches of blue that mottled the Ice Man's skin.

Fungus! The decomposers were already at work.

As I turned to shout the news to the man and woman waiting below, I caught sight of two others hurrying across the Boney Creek benchlands, arms waving overhead. A man and a boy. Their shouts and whoops finally reached us. My boy. And Raphael Tocco.

With all the grace I could muster, I clambered down from the bonfire and went out to meet them. On the way, I detoured far enough to retrieve Preston Waite's gun. Just a little precaution. I knew Jake would stick with me, no sweat. But Raphael Tocco was an unknown quantity. And, I hoped, unarmed.

25

Raphael Tocco reached me first. "What the hell is going on?" His glance moved beyond me and turned into an outraged stare after reaching Preston Waite. "And what in God's name have you done to Dr. Waite?"

Jake arrived at my side just as Raphael Tocco dashed off to comfort his mentor, who'd started bellowing again. "Mom, are you okay?" He clutched one of my arms with both of his trembling hands. "I heard those shots and started running."

Words to warm—and chill—a mother's heart. My son, the Good Samaritan, blessed with a courageous heart in an age that destroys heroes. Time for another lesson in what journalists like to term the harsh realities.

"I'm okay, sweetie." I patted his hands and

nodded toward Eleanor Demissov. "He shot Eleanor, but she's okay, too."

His mouth dropped open, and he looked from me to Eleanor to Preston Waite, and back again. I expected a bit of panic, but again Jake surprised me. "Why?"

I threw my arms around him and pulled him close. "God, I love you." He reared back, but not before I saw the smile kindled by my words. "I'll explain in a minute. In the meantime, stay close and listen up. I'm going to need your help."

As we walked toward the others, I realized that Jake was an asset in this situation, not the liability I might have feared. Although still a child in many ways, he wasn't helpless or hysterical. With any luck, he just might be my strong right arm.

Eleanor sat next to the bonfire she'd built, leaning against the lowest spruce branches for support. Raphael Tocco knelt before Preston Waite, muttering as he picked at the knots I'd tied in the strap securing his mentor. The old man continued to rave, sputtering in his eagerness to enlist his protégé's aid in "rescuing" his find.

I stopped a yard away from the men. "Don't untie him."

Raphael Tocco tossed a glare over his shoulder but still picked at the strap binding the old man. Preston Waite raved on. I was in no mood for such an affront to common courtesy. Jake's eyes widened when I drew my .45, but he didn't try to stop me. I pointed the pistol toward a nearby mesa and fired one round.

BLAM!

That got Raphael Tocco's attention. He leaped away from the old man, spinning after his launch, and wound up on his backside looking straight into the barrel of the Colt.

"Maybe you didn't hear me. I said, 'Don't untie him.' And I meant it."

Even the old man seemed cowed. He shut up, at least. Amazing the way a gun confers respect. Twisted, too, but for the moment useful.

"Here's what's happening." I lowered my hand until the .45 pointed at the ground but decided not to holster the gun. "A while back, Dr. Waite found a cave in the permafrost, and inside he discovered a man frozen in the ice. A very, very ancient man, perhaps as old as twenty-two thousand years."

At which news Raphael Tocco's mouth hung open, along with my son's. Preston Waite sputtered to life again. "At least twenty-two thousand B.P. and very likely much, much older. But I'll never know for sure unless you protect my find from that creature. Each moment you delay simply adds to the catastrophe."

I started to raise my gun, which proved to be enough to shut the old man up once again. "At some point, Belle Doyon probably made the same discovery. Dr. Waite tried to scare her off by leaving a couple of dead wolves at her door, but apparently that didn't work. So he shot her."

Raphael Tocco turned wide eyes on his mentor and at last found his voice. "You shot her? But why?"

The old man bristled with indignation. "I had no choice! You saw what they did to the artifacts from the Smithsonian. Buried beyond reach of those who would study them. I couldn't let that happen to my greatest find!"

I gave him a hard stare. "Neither Jake nor I posed any threat to your precious find, but you tried like hell to kill us, too."

Preston Waite's mouth flapped a couple of times but no words emerged. Apparently, verbal confrontation wasn't his style. The old man preferred guns.

I lifted a hand in Eleanor's direction. "And then Eleanor found the Ice Man."

"No." She shook her head slowly. "You found my ancestor while I followed."

Which meant my instincts weren't so hopeless after all. I'd sensed Eleanor's presence that evening but dismissed the sensation. I shrugged. "Whatever. What matters is that Eleanor decided her ancestor deserved a proper funeral. So she dug the Ice Man out of his cave and placed him on top of this pyre. Before she could torch the bonfire, Dr. Waite arrived and started shooting."

Raphael Tocco got to his feet and faced Preston Waite. "You tried to kill her, too? Is nothing more valuable than your reputation?"

Preston Waite gave a snort of disgust. "My God, Tocco, you must be mad. Didn't you hear what I said? Very likely older than twenty-two thousand B.P. Not a fragment. My find is whole. And perfectly preserved! What could be more valuable than that?"

Raphael Tocco turned away from the old man and studied the bonfire for a moment. "I'd like to see this Ice Man, if that's all right with you."

At my nod, he scrambled to the top of the spruce branches, and then Jake scurried up, too. Both knelt as I had, precariously balanced above the ancient man. Down below, no words were spoken, even after long minutes had passed. Finally, the pair atop the bonfire had seen enough and slid carefully to the ground.

Eleanor Demissov struggled to her feet and faced us all. "He was a man. And he is ancestor to the *Dene.*"

To my astonishment, Raphael Tocco took Eleanor's hand and nodded. "He was a man. And he deserves our respect."

Behind us, Preston Waite bellowed again. "My God, Tocco, you are mad! Come to your senses, man! This is the greatest find in the history of archaeology! In the history of the world!" The old man's voice cracked. "My God, Tocco, don't let that creature incinerate my find!"

Raphael Tocco had a good heart. So did my son. And in the end, Jake's words decided the Ice Man's fate. He took up position next to Eleanor Demissov, a twin guardian to Raphael Tocco on her other side. "Not just a man, Mom. He was a real person. Somebody's son. Somebody's friend. Maybe even somebody's dad."

I had to look away, then. Had to study the distant ridges that rose to the Kuskokwim Mountains and blink back my tears. Maybe the Ice Man really was like Max—just another traveler lost from his loved ones somewhere in the far reaches of the great land. And if one day a stranger happened across Max, no question what I would have him do.

Jake struck the spark that lit Eleanor's torch, but she alone touched off the Ice Man's funeral pyre. My son and I stood to one side while Raphael Tocco moved back to quiet and comfort Preston Waite. The spruce boughs caught quickly, hissing as sap boiled and snapping as pitch exploded. Flames licked up each side of the mound—higher, higher—until finally meeting in an arch above the ancient man. Then the fire blazed higher, reaching for the summer sky with a shower of sparks, and the Ice Man was no more.

26

This time I didn't have to face any pointed questions from Matt Sheridan. Or from any other cop, for that matter. The only person I had to face still lay in the ICU of an Anchorage hospital, struggling to recover from the grievous wounds inflicted by Preston Waite. So when Raphael Tocco asked for mercy for his mentor, I couldn't say yes and I couldn't say no.

"To say that he was a good man—that he is a great scientist—can't possibly atone for what he's done." He spread his hands in a gesture that matched his pleading eyes. "But how will locking him up for his last years serve the cause of justice?"

The young scientist found an unexpected ally in Eleanor Demissov, who inclined her head toward the smoldering embers of the Ice Man's funeral pyre. "The old one has been punished."

Even my own darling Jake chorused in with a plea for clemency. "He doesn't look too good, Mom. Going to jail might kill him."

In fact, Preston Waite already looked half-dead. As flames devoured the Ice Man, the fight leaked out of the old man, leaving him slumped against the rock like a rag doll, silent and staring. Try as I might, I couldn't stir up much rancor toward someone so broken and pathetic. Yet I couldn't forget what he'd done to my friend, either.

"Let's leave it up to Belle Doyon. If she wants him nailed, I'll make sure that happens. If she agrees with Eleanor, I'll leave him alone."

Unfinished business delayed our return to Anchorage for a couple of days. Jake wanted to help the Grandmother get in the last of her fish, so we stayed with Sarah Doyon until she convinced me that her supplies would last the winter.

"Such plenty, Lauren Maxwell!" Her eyes danced with merriment. "Fat fish means strong dogs, and ours will be the strongest in Tanana."

When I tried to give her a check to cover the cost of the boat we'd lost, she refused. "I have a boat."

"Yeah, but you used to have two. Before we sunk one."

The Grandmother shook her head. "I have all that I need."

A couple of days later, I repeated those words to her grandson when Jake and I stopped by John Doyon's office at TNC headquarters in Anchorage. "You may wonder who the hell I am to lecture you on the Athabascan lifeway, but I'll take the risk."

With all the smoothness of his Harvard M.B.A., he invited me to continue. "I respect your judgment."

"One thing I've always admired about the *Dene* is the way they take only what they need. Only enough fish to feed the dogs. Only enough moose to feed the family. For untold centuries, that ethic survived and so did the people."

"Barely." He frowned and sighed deeply. "For untold centuries, my people knew hunger. They expected to stand by helplessly while their children sickened and died."

To drive home his point, he raised a hand toward Jake, who fidgeted in a chair next to mine. "Life for my people was a short, brutal struggle against unbeatable odds."

I nodded agreement and leaned forward, resting an arm on his desk. "So now you want to help your people. As you should. My point is that you should never forget that original ethic—take only what is needed. That's an idea too much of the world has forgotten. We've confused what we want with what we truly need, and it's killing us."

For a second he actually looked surprised, but quickly recovered. "And your point is?"

Jake caught my eye, nodding encouragement. Not for the first time, I felt immeasurably bucked up by the presence of my son.

"Your business ethic demands maximum profit, so you want to fully exploit the aboriginal lands. But do your people truly need the income from the oil reserves on those subsistence lands?"

John Doyon's mouth curved into a half-smile. "You've been talking to Eleanor Demissov."

"Yes, I have. And so should you. You shouldn't confuse what you want with what your people need." I smiled, trying to soften the harsh words. "If Belle were here, she'd say the same thing."

John's half-smile widened into a grin. "She has and she will. I think all of her suffering succeeded in sharpening her tongue. Still, cutting words are much better than painful silence."

Maybe John's description scared Jake off. When we got to the hospital, he decided to stay in the family waiting room while I went into the ICU to see Belle. He whispered one final instruction before I left. "Don't forget to ask her about Dr. Waite. Once she decides, this really will be over."

In the space of a few days, the miracles had continued. I found my friend freed from the respirator and actually sitting up. She greeted me with a tired smile and a harsh croak. "Lauren."

Machines still whistled and beeped and buzzed, but her color had improved—hardly any yellow left—and several layers of bandages had been removed from her head. I came up beside the bed and laid my hand on the few square inches of her arm that weren't bruised from all the needles. "Don't talk if it hurts."

She nodded and relaxed against the pillow, closing her eyes. I thought she'd fallen asleep so I studied the machinery, reserving special attention for the heart monitor's electronic blip scrolling a jagged line to match the flub-dub of Belle's heart.

When I looked back at my friend, her dark eyes were open again and focused on me. I said the first thing that came to mind. "Do you hear your heart beating, almost like a slow drum?"

For a moment her eyes clouded. Then Belle Doyon nodded.

"The Grandmother said your dreaming would cure you."

The words brought the smile back to her face.

I matched her smile with one of my own. "The Grandmother is certainly one smart lady."

Again she nodded and then closed her eyes. I didn't say anything more, and not long after, tiptoed out of her room.

Outside the hospital a few minutes later, Jake reminded me of the mission I'd failed to accomplish. "So what did Belle say?" He jammed his hands into his jeans, trying to act casual. "About Dr. Waite?"

"Nothing." Before he could protest, I fudged the facts, just a bit. "She's not too concerned about him. She's concentrating on getting better."

Jake cocked his head and frowned. "Does that mean it's over?"

"Yup." I hooked my arm through one of his. Maybe now he could get back to being a kid. After all, he'd long since proved himself a man. "Let's go home."